THE DAY OF THE FERRET

Michael Woodman

Connlaswell Publishing

Copyright

First published in 2021 by Connlaswell Publishing.

Copyright © Michael Woodman 2021

Woodman, Michael. The Day of the Ferret. Connlaswell Publishing.

ISBN 978-1-9160095-7-8

The Brainstorm in the White House

January 25, 2019

Sitting in the Oval Office, Benny wrung his hands. The right one was trembling. No call for that. Earlier that day, one of the president's assistants had been arrested by the FBI. But so what? The federal indictment of a *very perfect man* surely hadn't led to a message like...

He checked his phone again.

URGENT. GET HERE NOW!

Since joining the president's legal team, assigned to the shitstorm portfolio, Benedetto Luigi Capone had gotten some strange messages from him, and although many had required an Enigma machine to decipher, he'd never had one like this. It wasn't just the correct spelling and syntax that troubled him. It was the tone. Aggressive was normal, but not aimed at him... and no clues on Twitter. That was always a worry. That meant it was something personal. God forbid he'd found out about the thundercloud rumbling along in Benny's wake. If he'd discovered that—

The door burst open, cutting short Benny's spiraling fears, and President John Thomas Rump strode into the room. Benny leapt to his feet and waited as the president dismissed a tail of flunkies with a staccato burst of imperatives: *do this, fire him...* the usual. So Benny didn't follow the detail on that part, his mind clouding darker... *something personal*... his hands still wringing, now hidden behind his butt. The door closed and the president swept by him, throwing out a last-minute high five on the way. A good sign, that, and so unexpected Benny nearly took it as a slap in the face. Quick reactions. That was what you needed with this guy, and flexibility since there was a good bit of bending over backwards and slithering through bolt-holes required. When Rump was settled behind the fabled desk, Benny sat in the visitor's chair, still nervous despite that high five.

"These accusations..." The president leaned forward, right fist balled in his left hand. "These women who—"

"I'm on top of it all, sir."

So that's all it was.

Benny's right hand finally came to rest.

"But what about the future? We need to be proactive, not reactive."

"Anyone particular in mind?"

"Something came up in a security briefing. NSA was checking out new software with twenty-twenty vision through any encryption. So they ran a test on the dark web looking for words like... *assassinate Rump*, being as that's such a popular search term at the moment, and they dug up a party I happen to know."

"They get a warrant yet?"

"They'll need a lot more than that. She's rich, and she's French."

Rump tossed a folded copy of the *Wall Street Journal* across the desk and Benny scooped it up. A news item had been marked up with expletives and a doodle that was either a rocket emerging from two puffs of smoke or a badly deformed penis. The headline read:

Offshore Fund behind CringR Dating App Linked to Reclusive Software Genius Coronata

Benny read the article and looked up.

"Eve Coronata?"

"She was in a beauty pageant back in Moscow..." Benny winced. *Please don't say Pee Tape*. "I kicked her out of the contest."

"Did you, eh...?" Benny's eyes went back to the newspaper, his eyes lingering on a rare photo of the elusive Madame Coronata.

"No way. She's a sore loser. That's all."

"Didn't the NSA get anything incriminating?"

"Not enough. She was sniffing around, trying to hook up with a super-assassin. The Ferret."

"So... if they keep listening, she'll dig her own grave."

The president shook his head. "She was using the nym Sea Urchin. But as soon as they found her, she dropped off the radar. It was like she knew they were onto her."

"Maybe she gave up."

"I doubt it."

"That's a long time to stay mad."

"They get heartbroken when I turn them down." Rump swept his hand back and forth across the blotting pad as if shooing away the dust of the past. "And who can blame them?" Benny had an answer to that but wisely kept it to himself. "Even if she can't find someone to shoot me, sooner or later, she'll shoot her mouth off."

"And say what?"

"Stuff... the usual."

That couldn't be right. If this was *the usual*, she could get in line with all the others.

Urgent. Get here now!

That wasn't usual. That was unique. Whatever this woman had on him, it had to be a career buster.

"So you want me to—"

"This one could really hurt me. If you can fix it... I swear, Benny. I'll kiss that sweaty bald head of yours until you love me."

Benny struggled a moment.

What kind of incentive is that?

"Maybe I could find some dirt on her so—"

"Invent it. Something very bad. What about money laundering? It says offshore."

Benny skimmed the article again, shaking his head. "That only works with criminal proceeds, and online dating is hardly..." His eyes caught an unrelated news item about a political killing in Croatia and it sparked a crazy idea. "How about assassination?" he said, chuckling. "If she's looking for an assassin, why not give her one?"

He looked up, expecting a counter-chuckle or a humorous riposte. But what he got was Rump leaping to his feet and pounding the desk with his fist.

"That's genius... frame her with a fake Ferret. If we nail her ass, it's a double whammy. We'll shut her down and skyrocket my shit ratings at the same time."

"Ratings?"

"Remember Ronnie?" Benny was beginning to see the noose he'd stuck his head into. Ronald Reagan had had the lowest approval ratings of any first-term US President until John Hinckley had shot him. Following that failed assassination attempt, Reagan's ratings had soared and he'd gone on to win a second term.

"Only"—the president frowned—"and this is an important point, the actual getting shot part... we'll need a workaround for that."

Benny frantically searched the lawyerspeak thesaurus in his head looking for *are you fucking crazy?* but all he could find was, "Sometimes ideas look good at first, but when you—"

Rump bashed the table again and lifted his eyes to heaven, chest burgeoning. "Son of a bitch... yes." He walked around the desk, picking up the bust of Winston Churchill on his way to the sofa. He waved for Benny to join him, and his lawyer sat in an armchair opposite, waiting as the president peered down at the storied British statesman nestling in his lap and thoughtfully stroked his brow.

"I can channel him," he said. "I found that out the other day by chance when I was doing this." He poked his finger into Churchill's ear and wiggled it around like he was wrestling a snail out of its shell. Benny looked on. No real way to comment on that. Whatever had gotten him poking the old boy's ears in the first place, Benny did not want to know. "Damn it!" Rump leapt up, holding the bust up high, his arms outstretched. "Thank you, sir." He replaced the bust on its stand and turned to Benny. "The fake Ferret trap... we'll spring it in France on D-Day." He swiveled back and tapped Sir Winston on the head. "That part was Winnie's... *stick it to the Frogs*, he said. He hated de Gaulle, you know." He shrugged. "That wife swap thing never works out." Benny nodded, his face taking on a sick pallor. He'd experimented with LSD once at college and as the president continued, he wondered if there was any link between that event and this conversation he appeared to be having with the leader of the free world. "All the haters will be there... Merkel." He made it sound like a disease you'd never recover from. "And that tight-ass British woman with the shoe thing—"

"Mrs. May."

"Yeah... and Macron." He ground that one out between his teeth.

"And you want me to...?"

"Put together a team. You've got four months. Create a trail that's easy for Coronata to find, then set up a trap for her."

Benny was getting the picture. He hadn't always been a two-thousand-an-hour lawyer. He'd grown up in the Bronx, where his father had been a mob enforcer, and he was still his father's son despite serving a term as New York's mayor. All he had to do was get some hacker to leave a trail leading Coronata to him, so she'd believe she was in contact with the Ferret instead of the president's personal attorney. Not easy, but not impossible for a man with his connections. Benny had prosecuted many hacking cases as a US attorney, so he was tech-savvy with a good grasp of the lingo. And what if it was crazy? Here was a shortcut to heavyweight brownie points with the president, and if things ever got rough, he'd have a sword of Damocles to dangle over his head. "If she's out sniffing," he said, "all my guys have to do is leave a trail of bread crumbs and—"

"Aren't ferrets meat eaters?"

Benny considered his options here before taking the easy way out. "Good point, sir."

"She's too smart to take any risk herself. She'll send a gofer."

"So we'll need a fall guy to meet with him, a snitch we can count on to rat them out—"

"Agreed... a total rat, a real creep."

"I'll get you the best, sir. Count on me."

Rump paced in silence before settling in his throne behind the presidential desk.

"Conspiracy to assassinate the president of the United States." He banged the desk and grinned, an orange glow lighting up his face. "How long will she get?"

"Long enough. But more to the point—no one will believe a word she says. She can talk any shit she wants and all the world will do is laugh."

"I'll be center stage... an *almost* victim of an assassination attempt by a French person. Macron will have to kiss my ass instead of his bodyguard's." He looked at Benny sharply. "You know about that, right? All I did was grab a few pussies and Macron's taking it up the—"

"It's the deep state thing." Benny threw it out like a reflex, desperate to head off the impending tirade. It was a bit of a stretch from Macron's ass to the president's groping, but that was the beauty of the deep state. It was infinitely flexible.

"Damn right, it is."

The president went quiet after that, signaling their session was coming to an end.

"So here's the bottom line." Benny always liked to finish on a high note. "Coronata goes to jail and no one believes her lies. You become a superhero who ducks an assassin's bullet and you get to piss on Macron's parade."

The president nodded, lowering his head as if imagining it all.

"You're a genius."

"Thank you, sir."

"And tell me, Benny, am I a man who keeps his promises?"

"Without fail, sir."

Rump strolled out from behind the desk and as Benny went to stand, he bade him stay put. The president walked around to the back of Benny's armchair, where he towered above him, and put his hands on Benny's shoulders. Benny tensed. Then his stony face twisted into a horror mask as the president's lips slid back and forth across his bald head in sweeping wet kisses.

Scurrying out of the Oval Office, Benny took refuge in the back of the limo. He'd survived another one-to-one with the president. But for how long? No one ever really knew. Playing on the president's team meant living life as a replicant with built-in obsolescence and a life span subject to daily updates.

So now this... a fake assassination.

And the timing was less than perfect. That Ukraine thing was going nowhere, and Benny's divorce was close to DEFCON 2.

The fall guy?

Everything depended on him. They'd need someone of unimpeachable dishonesty with a unique balance of desperation and stupidity. But how to find a loser like that? He could make a few calls. There were guys in intelligence who owed him. Benny was big on favors, the two-way kind. Once that was solved, he'd need a rat handler, someone to dupe the fall guy and set him up: a trickster, able to seduce and control men, someone treacherous whose back he had over a barrel.

The Witch of Switch.

Who else?

He pulled out his phone, eager to call her before he reached the helicopter, but it rang with an incoming call before he could dial out. He recognized the number, his lover's burner phone. Thank God she was using it—his wife's divorce lawyer would certainly subpoena his phone records.

"Ina," he cooed her pet name. She'd been throwing moods from hell lately and this was not the day for that.

"So?" she said, no cooed response.

"So... what?"

"Horndog." She let it hang there—the President's Secret Service codename—the dog part sliding out between clenched teeth from the sound of it. "What did he want?"

"Nothing... some bullshit. Hey, I'm heading back to Manhattan. I'm nearly at the heliport and I've got to make a call before—"

"Are you blowing me off?"

He rolled his eyes skyward.

Why today? Why now?

"*Mia innamorata*..." He crooned it in Bronxified Italian. *La lingua dell'amore* hit her button every time, and he soon had her laughing, then talked her off the phone.

The limo was pulling into the heliport by then. He'd have to be quick.

"It's me—" he said, as soon as the call went through, but the auto-attendant cut him short. "Damn." Benny listened, patience draining, pressure building. *Hi, loser... can't get to the phone right now, too busy whipping a scumbag like you...* All that groveling Benny had had to do around the president had taken a toll on his attitude towards lesser mortals. So to combat this creeping malaise with its unlawyerly side effects like shaking people by the throat, Benny had gotten a therapist who'd prepared him for stress points like this with ten surefire techniques to control his temper. *Either that, or I'm just not picking up because I want to listen to your whiny cravings while my slave here eats my toenails.* Benny was working through the list, rejecting them one by one as he tried to get that toenail thing out of his head. Most were guaranteed to make him more angry and one—*don't hold a grudge*—culturally offensive to an Italian. *Leave a message. You may get lucky... meanwhile, why don't you hold your breath? It's a real turn-on when you go blue.*

"Hey, Felicity, it's me. Remember when the prosecutor lost that file on you? Anyway... he just found it. So you better call me back pronto. Either that, or get yourself an orange onesie. You're going to need it." He hung up, grinning, frustration gone. *Be mean* wasn't on the therapist's list, a clear omission as it was outrageously effective.

The limo screeched to a halt and he hurried to the helicopter, his thoughts flipping back to his beloved Ina. He strapped himself in, adjusted the noise-canceling earphones, and stared blindly out the window as his thoughts drifted into dreams.

How much he wanted her, longed to make her his own. But realistically, what were the chances of that? How had it even happened?

She was younger and unspeakably beautiful. But that wasn't it. There were plenty of others who fitted that bill. It was that special thing she had, that sullen Slavic nasty bitch thing. It made his flesh tingle, and his... He sighed and closed his eyes.

Too bad she's the president's wife.

PART 1 - May 2019

A Scoundrel, a Witch, a Wrestler and a Setup

Four thousand miles from Washington, the once-and-future fall guy leapt out of bed.

No... wait.

He crawled out. But in his own mind, it was a leap. That was the kind of man Gatlin was—deluded. And in fairness to his judgment, it was an unusually fast crawl. So it took him a moment to recover, wobbling, dizzy and naked in the dark.

"What is it?" Brunhilda sat up, flicking on the bedside lamp.

"You didn't hear it?" he said, blinking.

"Now you're awake, let's try again. I wanted tonight to be special because—"

"There's someone out there."

"It's just the plumbing. These Spanish houses are built like *scheiss*. Come on..." She patted the bed. "I'm sure you can do better this time."

The scream of a chainsaw cut her short and drowned out the crickets, chirping in the stillness of the early summer night.

"Those sons of bitches." Gatlin grabbed a golf club from the bedroom closet and ran through the villa and out into the garden via the back door. He stopped, club at the ready.

There they are...

A bunch of denim-clad bandits were hoisting their booty over the wall, his prime pot with the latest Dutch-

Colorado genetics. He screeched and charged, brandishing his club and even more frighteningly his nakedness, with his belly swinging one way and his dick the other in some bizarre anatomical symmetry. But his fearsome attack was short-lived. He stopped with a groan, nearly toppling over, his eyes dropping to the white stones at his feet. Low maintenance. That was what they called the garden. No dirt. No lawn. Just carpets of white stones, and not foot-friendly pebbles either, but chips of rock with razor-sharp edges. The groan turned into a sigh as he looked up and saw the last of the men disappearing over the wall. The roar of an engine told him the rest. The culprits were gone, and he would never catch them. Those ripe buds destined to reinvigorate the lives of ailing seniors in his cannabis social club would instead put va-va-voom in the sex lives of teenagers. He tiptoed back to the villa to avoid the brutal stones and stopped at the door, rooted by his own image. Brunhilda had turned on the terrace lights. So he could see his reflection in its plate glass.

Who's that pathetic old man?

Only yesterday, he'd been a cocky young London lout selling his skills as a break-in specialist and black bag man to MI6.

Now look!

An aging gigolo, peddling pot to pensioners and—

The door opened and Brunhilda appeared in the doorway.

"You'd better come in," she said. "I've got something to tell you."

They sat at the table in the kitchen. She'd made coffee and Gatlin had thrown on his pants and a sports shirt. Best not to be naked at a moment like this. He knew what was coming. *The chop*. She'd been signaling it for weeks, drip-feeding him clues. Yes, she still called him *darlink*, but where once she had murmured it like Marlene Dietrich, now she squawked it like R2-D2.

"It's over," she said in full-blown droid mode.

He gave her a pained look.

"I can grow a new crop," he said, feigning misunderstanding. "There's plenty of summer left for—"

She slapped her hand down on the table. "Enough. The summer is not the problem. The pot thieves are not the problem. You and me is the problem."

"If this is about what happened earlier,"—he nodded down at his crotch—"that kind of thing—"

"And it's not about Little Gatlin." In the circumstances, her use of that pet name didn't help much. "I talked to my *abogado*, my lawyer, and he tells me that..." She stopped and played with the lapels of her robe like she was getting comfortable. But he'd seen it all before. Not only had he gotten the live show, but he'd seen the original in the seventies movie that had launched her brief career as the Berlin Bombshell. She smoothed her lapels before looking up, and as they fell apart in a revealing exposé, she delivered the big line. "You lied to me. You don't have a Cannabis Social Club license." Gatlin went to speak, but she hushed him into silence with a sweep of her hand. "You have turned my home into an illegal pot farm. What would Hermy say?" Herman, the so-called widget king of Wankendorf, was her late husband, the bonus payout from her fifteen minutes of fame, a rich man in need of a trophy wife. "I could lose my house."

"The application's being processed. You know how slow they are in Spain."

She ignored him and checked her phone.

"Your taxi's here."

"My taxi...? But I need that car. I can't—"

"Keys." Her hand shot out. Gatlin stayed rigid, his face stony. This was way worse than he'd imagined. "I wanted our last night to be special. But sometimes things happen like this for the best. Of course, the taxi is on my account." He gave her the keys, and she smiled as she slipped them in her pocket.

What about those wonderful times, etc.?

The words were at his lips, but he was too crestfallen to get them out. It wasn't so much losing her. That was a relief in a way. But the pot heist. That was a seismic disaster. It had taken all the fight out of him. So he left her and made his mournful way to the gate. It buzzed open and he stepped out onto the road where he stood surveying the empty street as the gate rolled shut behind him.

What taxi?

He stuck his thumb on the intercom button and left it there but soon gave up. There was a mute switch on the comms panel in the hallway. He'd often used it when Jehovah's Witnesses had rung looking for aging expats to fleece.

Damn it...

How many times had he been here?

Not right here in front of this villa, but right here in his life. Someone had once told him that a man's fate was like a game of backgammon, a fifty-fifty split between a dice roll and a decision, and what separated winners from losers was not the dots on the dice but the moves made with them.

So how come mine are always wrong?

He headed down the road, bravado straightening his back. He faced a long walk down to the coast, where he'd have to wait for a bus, and to heap misery on chagrin, the wind had come up. No pussyfooting breeze either, but that blast that turns up at dawn wherever mountains reach the sea. He stopped after a bit, sitting on a wooden bench. According to its metal plaque, some old man had bequeathed it in memory of his wife, having enjoyed the view from this spot with her. It was a fine view too, white villas clinging to craggy canyons, green threads of vegetation running all around them, and beyond it all the sea. The bench was on a plot of land left wild and overgrown with pines. It was one of the green areas that peppered the urbanization, providing poo spots for the residents' pampered pooches. Gatlin found a stub of a spliff in his pocket and lit it up with difficulty, finally firing up his aging Zippo in the shelter of the dog poo bin next to the bench. Seated comfortably again, he puffed, savoring the taste of his previous crop, oblivious to the far more robust odors coming from the bin, which had clearly not been emptied for weeks. And so, while quietly reflecting on his fate, he fell asleep...

Ruff-ruff-ruff—

Gatlin felt a tug on his jeans and lashed out his foot. There was a yelp and he opened his eyes to see a dog that looked like a rat with a bad haircut go zinging across the road and bounce at the feet of a large blond woman. It was so surreal, dogs flying and all, that Gatlin dismissed it as part of a dream, and it was only when the woman approached him screaming, with the rat dog clutched to her breasts, that Gatlin realized he was awake. The wind had picked up during his nap and it was creaking through the pines and blowing most of what she said back in her face. But some of her hollering got through. Bits were in English and bits in some other language—Dutch, maybe, or one of those Scandinavian languages spoken by about six and a half people. Gatlin wanted to howl back, to give her a good dose of his rage, but the words *police* and *drugs* soon put an end to that. His eyes flashed on the remnants of his joint, now extinguished, but still clinging to his fingers. Local laws permitted homegrown cannabis to be consumed privately and nonprofit clubs to share weed with their members, but public smoking was a crime, and one that might lead to awkward questions about his own distinctly for-profit club. He reached to the side and buried the evidence in the doggy-doo bin, a risky endeavor, but as expected, the dog owners in this classy neighborhood had bagged their turds prior to disposal. Gatlin surveyed his hand as he pulled it out, noting with regret that not all of them were that classy. He got off the bench, wiped his hand on the grass, then sniffed at it tentatively by way of a quality control check before giving it another wipe.

Can things get worse than worst?

Grammarians be damned.

You bet they can!

As the woman scurried off, Gatlin trudged onward until—

Thwack... a loud sound made him stumble.

He whirled around, holding his chest to calm his pounding heart. The bench had been crushed by a windblown branch, a log more like. It had smashed through the planks right where he'd been sitting. He stood staring at it, struck dumb by the sequence of events. If that dog hadn't... if that woman hadn't... There was no other interpretation. If that angelic dog hadn't woken him up, and if that blessed woman hadn't scared him into hiding his spliff in the dog shit bin...

He looked up to the heavens, his hands joined in gratitude. It was the same sky he'd been cursing only moments before. But back then, it had been mundane, clouds and blue bits. Now it was biblical. Only an idiot would not read this as a sign. He was reborn. One last chance. The dice had been rolled and this time he was going to read the numbers right. There had to be something around the next bend, something good, something great.

I wonder what?

TWO

As Gatlin was relishing his new take on life, on the other side of the Atlantic, Benny Capone was at the kitchen table of his Manhattan apartment, flicking ash from a cigar on the remains of a half-eaten Szechuan takeout. He was waiting for the VPN to connect, the virtual private network that would conceal his activities on the dark web. Today was the day. The clincher, the signing off, the green light launching the genius plan. It had to happen now. He had to ratchet up the pressure. The president had been kicking his ass demanding updates, and Benny's bullshit battery was running low. So far, everything had gone as planned. His pet hacker had laid the trail in zeros and ones, and Eve Coronata had sniffed her way into the trap. But there was a problem. Benny was impersonating the Ferret, and she wanted proof that he was for real. Somehow she'd gotten forensic information about the Ferret's previous work, probably from some bent French cop, and had posed a series of questions that only the Ferret could answer. Benny logged in to the encrypted chatbox and glanced at the restricted access NSA file the president had shared with him.

Here goes nothing.

He typed the word RICIN.

According to the file, the Ferret had used this poison to assassinate an exiled Russian dissident. It was the answer to her most recent question. Three questions, and now she had three correct answers. Benny had delivered the goods, thanks to the president's access to pretty much any information available anywhere.

Benny waited, then added, IS IT GO OR NO?

He drilled the words into the laptop with stubby one-finger pokes.

Her reply was instantaneous.

GO

Benny licked crusted morsels of Szechuan sauce from the corners of his mouth and hit the keys again, their conversation moving on to the good faith payment, where his refusal to accept crypto was a stumbling block. But in the end, she agreed to his demand for an old-fashioned cash transaction between go-betweens. Benny had no choice about that. Cash changing hands and a gofer linked to her were essential to a successful sting. That first payment would pass without incident. But on the big money day, on the eve of the assassination, the FBI would pounce. That was the plan, and a real-life chain of bodies that led back to Coronata was the crux of it.

When the details were fixed, Benny cut the connection, rekindled his cigar and enjoyed a few puffs. He was scheduled to see the president the following day. He'd save the good news until then, but the Witch had to be told right away. Besides, she'd have news of her own. She was already in Europe and she should have recruited the gofer by now. Benny had tapped his owes-me-a-favor network, and a former CIA agent he'd kept out of jail had recommended the perfect patsy, Gatlin Fry, a Brit whose MI6 dishonorable discharge papers described him as a consummate loser. His former employers had said a lot of other things about him too. But most of that had been redacted to comply with UK obscenity laws.

Benny's phone buzzed with an incoming message. His wife, *el bitcho*. He knew it was her without looking. He'd assigned her a custom alert tone, Pink's divorce anthem, "So What," and most days he got a kick out of ignoring her calls and singing along with the *na-na-na-na-na-na* chorus. But she'd found a lawyer with a personal grudge against Benny, someone on the I'll-sue-Capone-for-free network that had exploded on the day he'd signed on with Rump. He'd sicced a team of forensic accountants and investigators on Benny and served up papers with a gruesome new twist to their who gets what battle. *Na-na-na-na-na-na* was coming back to haunt him. He read the message to shut it up. More demands and threats. *How did they find out this stuff?* He scrolled through page after page of it, stopping occasionally to snort with derision. As his finger swiped, his anger grew, his better self struggling to recall one of his therapist's ten techniques.

Number five.

Get some exercise.

That was as far as he got when his mind went blank with rage.

He pounded the remains of the Chinese takeout with his fists until he ran out of wind and fell exhausted in the mess of crumpled boxes, sauce, and mashed food seasoned with ash. He lay in this culinary swamp, heaving on air and waiting for his heart to drop out of the cardio zone. Then he pulled himself up and wiped his hands on his shirt. It was ruined. One of his last good ones too, handmade by a former client and his go-to tailor back in the days when he was mayor of New York. *Good old Mo*. Too bad about his indictment—not much call for sea-island cotton tailoring in FCI Otisville.

Benny stood up, his anger spent.

Who'd have thought it?

Exercise.

That dumb therapy shit had actually worked.

In Paris, Zaza Hasan knew nothing about that encrypted exchange between his boss, Eve Coronata, and the faux-Ferret. But he was about to find out, albeit in a roundabout way. He stepped into her office. Madame's company occupied the entire penthouse of the Tour Mars, the seventh-tallest building in Paris, and her private office was close to half of that, its floor-to-ceiling windows looking down on a toy town cityscape that stretched forever. Eve Coronata was taking in that view as he entered. She was standing with her back to him, the filtered sunlight framing her silhouette and catching the saffron of her cashmere-silk jumpsuit, the one she'd bought off a model's back at some fashion show. He'd been sitting next to her when she'd bought it. Sitting, standing, walking, it didn't matter. Whatever she was doing, Zaza was next to her. Bodyguard was his job title, but she preferred minder, and so did he. The total care package. That was his job. Minding was the big picture. He took care of everything, or almost. One part was missing. He often thought about that missing part. How nice it would be to...

"Madame." He stood motionless, waiting.

"Did you pack?" She didn't turn around.

"Yes, Madame, but I—"

"A few things is all you'll need. An overnight bag."

"Yes, but—"

"I didn't tell you *where* for a reason." She whirled around to face him. "But I will."

"Now?"

"On the way to the jet." She headed for her dressing room. "I need to change. I'll see you downstairs."

Forty-five floors and thirty minutes later, the armored limo pulled out of the Tour's underground lot at a fast clip, always the fast clip, like a prime minister or a president. Zaza barked out instructions to the driver, then closed the Bentley's partition window, sealing them in its leather-upholstered backseat cocoon.

"Before I tell you where," she said, "I have to tell you why." Zaza sucked up a groan and forced a smile. How could he protect her if he didn't know where they were going and what threats they faced? "But since *why* is such a long story, I'm going to give you the elevator edition. You know how sometimes I get upset when I check Twitter because—"

"POTUS."

"Oh... you figured it out already."

Figured it? He'd had daily demos since before the US elections. Even a mention of Rump's name was enough. The John Thomas, as she called him, only had to be alluded to for his dignified, classy, overeducated and unspeakably beautiful employer to start banging and smashing things.

"Well...," she continued, "it's grown into a plan."

"What has?"

She took her time with that, her eyes flickering onto the Paris streets speeding by. He waited. It had started to rain, a drizzle from a leaden ceiling of clouds.

"Rage," she said, getting back to his question and gate-crashing his daydream. "My rage against him."

"The John Thomas?"

"*That* is what has grown... once it was just an emotion. Now it's an actionable plan."

Actionable?

Zaza stuck his hand in his pocket, reaching for his comfort hankie. His mother had given it to him as a child to stop him crying in the dark, but noting his use of it—prior to a championship bout—when he'd grown into a three-hundred-pound, six-foot-three-inch wrestler, she'd taken it off him, making him so angry he'd broken both his opponent's arms.

"More. I'm underselling it," she went on. "It's a project. No, wait. A campaign... a cataclysm." She spread her arms dramatically, like there was a vista opening up before them. Zaza wasn't too sure about the word *cataclysm*, but he got the drift. As for that imaginary vista, all he could see was trouble. "The time has come," she said, "for me to settle my account with the US president."

"We're going to America?"

"Spain. This is just the first step. We have to make a payment in cash to get the ball rolling."

"Rolling where?"

"That's the tricky part. This is way outside your"— she adjusted her jacket, his eyes getting dragged to her splayed breasts and the butterfly tattoo inked between them. *Evenus Coronata*, she'd once told him, the world's most beautiful butterfly—"job description."

Zaza let out a long breath. It was that time again, the Beverly moment, when he'd remind himself he was a married man and had a wife to consider. Once, Beverly had been his dream girl, everything he'd lusted after as a lad growing up on a farm in Turkey. And their first encounter had been pure Hollywood, with Beverly playing the drunk Brit who decks a haughty French waiter in a dispute over a bar bill. It was love at first sight for Zaza—a brawling Amazon with a D-cup and fearsome combination punches. But all that had changed when she'd found God, or, to be more precise, Allah. Zaza had never been a regular at the mosque—just once or twice a year when his father's tongue had reached down all the way from paradise to give him a lashing. But when she'd googled *starting out in Islam*, he'd encouraged her at first.

What a mistake!

The booze was the first thing to go. No more sleazy soirees of gross obscenity kicked off with extra-strong lager and fueled by hookahs of military-grade hashish. Then she'd started rationing sex, reducing his quota to certain days a month when she was likely to conceive. Now sex was all about procreation, not fun. And that wouldn't have been so bad if it weren't for her physical transformation. Hours a day spent reading the Koran had mysteriously shifted her weight from her tits to her ass, and she'd ditched her entire come-hither wardrobe in favor of a black tent. As for makeup, that was now unnecessary as she'd taken to wearing a burka full time. She even slept in it. After marrying a life-size Barbie on steroids, he'd ended up in bed with Darth Vader. Even the allotted fuck-days were joyless. He'd get no prior notice, just a last-minute alert with her jacking up her tent, bending over the kitchen table and saying, "Get on with it." Desperate to escape his fate, he'd doubled down on her obsession. If she was in love with Allah, there was no way to get her back. So why not inch her along the path to the very end? With that in mind, he'd been encouraging her to join ISIS, even offering to buy her a one-way ticket to Syria. Current status? She was mulling it over.

"So who's the payment to?" he said.

"A unique man."

"And what's he going to do for us?"

"Assassinate President John Thomas Rump."

Gatlin was sitting in his caravan, in what his American friends, if he'd had any, would call a trailer, or more likely a really shitty trailer. Yes, this was his home. This was what his threescore years of life had accomplished.

Zip, zilch, nada.

He had no money. Not even a pension. Or barely any. Those scumbags at the pension office had found a loophole to wiggle out of paying him, something about never having worked or paid any contributions. He'd explained the reason for that, his background as a top-secret MI6 agent. But they'd remained unimpressed, even going so far as to question his credentials and get security to chuck him out on the street. Vistamar Camping, his humble abode, was in Benidorm on Spain's Costa Blanca. Of course, there was no *vista* of the *mar*. The view from his stained windows was of scruffy trailers and the sad losers who occupied them. He reached for his bong, took out his last bud, chopped it fine and stuffed it in the bowl.

Puff-puff.

What next? There was only one option. Another woman. Not a German this time. They were way too practical. Too smart by half. His thoughts wandered back to that ghastly Brunhilda bedroom incident. How she'd kept yanking his wanger and saying *vy is the blue pill not vorking*, a miserable scene that soon morphed into a horror show when she'd grabbed a flashlight to get a closer look. How humiliating was that? *Yank-yank-yank*. His spotlit dick wobbling in her frenzied grip under the glare of a high-power beam, looking for all the world like a throttled turkey. *Turn it off*, he'd snapped. But that had only made it worse. She'd fumbled the buttons, and a moment later, the whole sad scene was bathed in an SOS strobe light.

No more Germans. Maybe Spanish. Gatlin bemoaned his poor grasp of the language. But if Spain was the wrong country, it was the right idea. A Latin woman. Someone with a heart full of passion, enough to blind her to the reality that he was old, unattractive, overweight, and widely thought of as a chiseling worm of a man. He stood up and checked himself out in the mirror. It was the oddest thing. In selfies, he looked old and worn, a coffin-dodger on borrowed time. But he looked good in this mirror, one of those older men that the world had blessed with seasoning rather than wear and tear. So which image was the real Gatlin Fry, the mirror or the selfie? He did his coy smile, hitching up the left side of his mouth. A lover had once told him it made him irresistible.

Not too far!

He'd overdone it. That rotten eyetooth was a real turnoff. If only he could afford American teeth, he could get any woman he wanted.

French.

That was the answer. A French woman. He still had a schoolboy command of the language and the frogs were swarming all over the Costa Blanca, sucked into the vacuum left by Brexit-bound Brits. He checked the closet's contents. He still had some decent clothes. He went back to the friendly mirror, slapping his belly and heaving it up a bit. It wasn't so big, relatively speaking, although he'd have to nix a few full-English breakfasts.

So that was the plan...

Find a place where rich old French broads hung out and pick one with a little belly of her own, so she couldn't disqualify him on that basis. Then—

The trailer door burst open. It was a dramatic event. Not one of those turn the handle and open nicely jobs, but *wham, bam, here comes the SWAT team*. One second it was closed. The next it was open. And there was a *whoosh* too, and a cloud of ethereal matter—smoke to you peasants—oozing in from the darkness. No, that last part didn't happen. The door opened with a bang alright. But the smoke thing was Gatlin's fantasy, a coat of pot-powered whimsy etched onto the drama.

Gatlin stood immobilized.

What an entrance!

Who? What? How?

He was bursting to know. The aforementioned SWAT team was a prime candidate. But surely, Brunhilda wouldn't have ratted him out for... well, pretty much anything and everything.

So who?

A woman appeared as if by magic. A single step and she was there. Not so much a woman as a goddess. She was standing in the doorway, legs astride, boots planted so resolutely that she looked like a runaway truck wouldn't budge her.

"Sit down," she said.

He reeled in shock, a series of retorts zooming around in his head but never finding his mouth. *Who the hell are you? What a bloody cheek... this is my caravan.* Stuff like that for the most part. But all that came out of him was a grunt. Not even, more like a whimper. She pointed at him, aiming her index finger like a lethal weapon and it was impossible to miss the stiletto of a fingernail poking off the end.

"I said... sit." He didn't want to, but he did, following through like a knee tapped by a doctor's hammer.

He went to the table in the dining area and slid onto the bench seat. She closed the door and sat opposite him. That gave him time to recover somewhat, but he still wasn't sure how to react. On the one hand, there was the prideful stuff—the admonitions—and on the other hand, the reality stuff. Only moments before, he'd been speculating on an uncertain future in pursuit of a wealthy French woman with a matching belly and poor dental hygiene. But here was the present. Not French, but American, more ma'am than madame. She looked like she was loaded too, and what a bonus, that bod, a dribblefest of womanhood.

A briefcase appeared on the table and her hands buzzed, strong nails rolling tumblers and reaching inside.

Money.

A bundle of euros. She leaned forward and held it between them, her elbows on the table, the brick of notes equidistant between them. It was all too much for Gatlin, and his circuitry hit overload. Her hypnotic green eyes, that tasty wad, and flashing in and out of frame as she waved it, her cleavage, breasts nestling on the table, their burgeoning bulge and teasing retreat as she rocked back and forth staging an irresistible peep show.

"My name is Felicity Drillbit," she said. "My enemies call me the Witch of Langley, and my friends call me Felix. But you can call me *sir*." She put the money on the table and pushed it towards him, her breasts consuming his reality with volumes of subtext. "I'm going to transform your world. So listen carefully, my little man..."

THREE

Benny was in the shower, learning how hard it was to wash off the stink of Szechuan sauce, when he remembered what he'd forgotten.

Felicity, the Witch... he cursed himself.

He should have made that call by now. Instead, he'd had a food fight with himself. That message from his wife, those papers from her lawyer, he could have ducked all that by getting an attorney instead of representing himself. *Pro se*... that's what lawyers called it, and it was always a dumbass thing to do. But the thought of handing over money to a divorce lawyer made him feel physically sick. Attorneys were all such goddamn crooks, and now she'd hired the best. He put on his bathrobe and retrieved his phone from the kitchen, taking care not to step in any of the sauce splotches peppering the floor. Back in the lounge, he put the call through.

"Who are you?" a male voice answered Felicity's phone.

"Who am I? Who the hell are you?"

The answer came after a pause, the words thick with an accent he couldn't place and enunciated slowly like the revelation of a state secret. "I am the person who is answering this phone."

Benny resisted the urge to explode, the image of the kitchen war zone still fresh. "I get it. You're the wise guy she got from Bulgaria." He'd given Felicity a number, a friend of a guy he hadn't put in jail when he was a prosecutor, following a generous donation to his offshore charity. "You're the muscles from... what's that place called? Soufflé?"

"Very funny. You are funny man. Hello, funny man... dummy man. I am Dimitar Kohary of the House Saxe-Coburg. I am cousin to the tsar of Bulgaria, and you bullshit me!"

"Tsar? How did that royalty thing work out under the Soviets?"

"Not well."

"And how about the EU?"

"Much better... we have our own Instagram page."

"I remember now... she calls you Dimo, right?"

"No... *Dee-mo*, not *Dim-o*. And why she tell you about me?"

"Because I'm the Mr. Very-Important-Person who gives her the money she gives to the tsar of Bulgaria's cousin. What d'you think about that, Dim-o?"

Another long pause.

"Greetings, sir."

"So where is she?"

"With Wingnut."

"Who's that?"

"The falling man."

Benny took a second to interpret.

"The fall guy. Fry. She calls him Wingnut? Why? Has he got extreme political views... like a fanatic? I didn't even know that. It makes him perfect."

"No... not fanatic, just big ears."

Bit of a downer, that... a crazy leftist profile would've been perfect.

"So why'd she leave the phone with you?"

"She took special phone for him. This one fall out of her bag on seat."

"Tell her Coronata is on the way and tell her to call me."

Benny rang off and went to the kitchen, stopping in the doorway to survey his handiwork. He wanted some coffee, but no way was he going to navigate that mess. He went back to the lounge and picked up his phone. He'd remembered the name of a female divorce lawyer who'd had spectacular success protecting the fortunes of her male clients, who included Hollywood stars and Silicon Valley billionaires. He sat with his phone, his fingers hovering over it. She'd rape him financially. That was a given. She was a lawyer. Surrender to his wife's demands, that was a cheaper option. But then, she'd *na-na-na-na-na* all the way to the bank, an unbearable thought. Benny stared at the phone, fingers quivering, mind spinning.

Zaza and Eve were still in the Bentley enroute to the airport, so there was time to bail if he'd heard that wrong. It had sounded like... *assassinate the president of the United States*, as in *welcome to Lee Harvey Oswald country*. That couldn't have been right. Eve Coronata was not only one of the richest women in the world, she was one of the smartest. So she couldn't be that dumb. She couldn't let rage blind her common sense. Zaza had no idea what her beef with Rump was, but it wasn't his fight, and as a Muslim, albeit of frail faith, he knew that picking a fight with the US president was like signing up for a day trip to Guantanamo Bay. But how to break the news?

"Did you say—?"

"It's not as crazy as it sounds, and your role will not put you in danger. But before I fill in the blanks, I want you to tell me your dream."

"Why?"

"Because I'm going to make your dream come true. Whatever it is. You've got it, if you just help me with this."

His dream? Way too easy... a villa in Bodrum, Turkey's St. Tropez, and a harem of sleazy blondes to share it with. And how about an infinity pool and a slip down in the marina with a yacht waiting to whisk his harem off to the Greek islands?

"Well?" Eve prompted.

"A little cottage by the sea," he said after a quick edit. Madame Coronata had not struck him as a rampant feminist. Nonetheless, the raw reality of his dream, the naked shot with no rose-colored tint to filter out its testosterone surplus, might not sit well with her.

"For you and Beverly?"

"And a little boat, so I can catch her some fish."

Eve sighed, her hands crossing on her breasts like she'd seen a holy vision.

"How beautiful." She snapped her fingers. It was a good snap too, loud and resonant, the sort of snap a construction worker leaning on a bar would have been proud of. "It's yours. I'm not up to speed on real estate costs in Turkey, but would five million be enough?"

"Turkish lira?"

"Don't be silly. Euros." All he could do was splutter, his words mashing together and fading into a deep-throated gurgle. "Agreed?"

He nodded, still wordless, although not thoughtless. His yes was for the euros, but he still had a no up his sleeve for the killing of a US president.

"So we trade dreams."

They shook hands. It was brief—a single shake—but she held on tight, her frail white fingers dragging his hairy paw back to her lap. He didn't resist, although he knew he should have. She was the touchy-feely type, and she sometimes forgot that he was a married man. His hand nestling in her lap entwined with hers made him feel giddy like all the oxygen had been sucked out of the car. He'd never felt anything like it before. Not even with Beverly in her heyday. It was such a special feeling, like—he had to search to find it—like eating his mother's meatballs. He'd eaten Turkey's celebrated *içli köfte* all over the country, but none came close to his mother's. That blessed woman had some magical spice in her soul that transformed her meat into ambrosia. His pulse raced. Yes, Eve Coronata, she had it too, the *içli köfte* spice. He struggled to quiet his racing heart. "And your dream," he said, a sudden draft of doom chilling his ardor, "is... killing the president?"

"Yes." She hefted his meaty paw to her face and kissed it. "And you're going to help me do it."

He pulled his hand back, not sharply, and with some regret. However spicy she was and however much she paid him, no way was he going to do a Lee Harvey Oswald.

"Yours is such an ambitious dream," he said. "Do you think it could be too ambitious?"

"It's a matter of honor. He damaged my soul."

"But I've never actually killed anyone. In the police, I was more of a half-killing-them specialist. Actual killing is a big step up. And the president? That's like leaping over the moon. I don't think I could—"

"You don't have to kill anyone. We're hiring someone to do that—an assassin."

"But why?"

"I can't speak of that. It's too painful."

"I don't want to refuse, but—"

"If I tell you, you'll judge me and—"

"No, I won't. I respect and admire you. I've done some things I'm not proud of too. We all have."

She eyed him speculatively. "I met the John Thomas a long time ago."

"So tell me the story."

He could read the hesitancy in her eyes. But then she said, "Once upon a time, I was young and innocent, and"—she drew a long breath—"the jet's waiting."

"What?"

The Bentley rolled to a halt next to the jet. She was right. Its engines were whining. He caught her wrist as she turned towards the door.

"Another day," she said, and he let her go. "They'll be a right time. I know it."

A thousand miles to the south, Gatlin was fishing for information too.

"You're with the CIA?" he said, casting his mind back. He recalled one or two operations involving American agents. He couldn't pin down the specifics, but he took it as read that he'd ripped them off at some point. But enough to send an asset after him all these years later? Hardly. Especially not one with the class of Felicity Drillbit. "But why do they call you *the Witch of Langley?*"

"Because I've been modified. I have implants."

His eyes zoomed in on her breasts.

"Oh no…" She waved her hand in front of them. "They're real. I'm talking about these." Her fingernails were inches from his eyes, curved talons painted with the stars and stripes. Gatlin watched hypnotized as her hand dropped to his and she scoured off a layer of his skin. CIA weaponized nails. He squeaked and stared in horror at the blood oozing out of his striated flesh. "Titanium. I could gut you like a fish. And I've been genetically reengineered too. Do you know what pheromones are?"

Gatlin snorted. He had no idea. "Of course I do."

"Mine have been recalibrated to tap into the lizard brains of men. It's a psycho-hack. One whiff of me and I'm jacked into their libido. Once there, I have total control of them." That sounded wild, and even to Gatlin's fried brain a little farfetched. On the other hand, times had moved on since his day, and he'd seen a Bourne movie with something similar, so it was probably true. "Do you understand what I'm saying?"

Gatlin nodded, pleased to be keeping up.

"You're controlling my brain with your vagina."

"I'm impressed." She smiled. "You're smarter than they told me."

"But why me?"

"Computer says…" She sang it out like a synthesized voice.

"What?"

"You put data in, the computer chews on it, then spits out the answer."

"The computer picked me?"

"You were way out in front. We wanted a scumbag, someone who'd steal from his own mother. Only it turns out that the world's full of them. Our ideal candidate needed more. He had to be a serial loser too, someone guaranteed to shoot himself in the foot every time he pointed a gun at someone's head."

"And it chose me?" Gatlin was desperate to get the win. It wasn't the most salubrious of events, but a first is a first whatever the race.

"Poles ahead, darling..."

"And the money?"

"Yours. Consider it a down payment."

He was about to ask for what—but why bother? He had the picture. They needed a scumbag. He could do that. He was a natural. He reached for the cash reflexively, like a gecko gobbling a fly, but she slapped his hand away.

"Your job is to trap a crazy woman who's trying to kill the president of the United States."

"Why does she want to kill him?"

"Who cares? Something way back. She wants to hire an assassin."

"Me?" He almost choked on the word.

"Don't be an idiot." Gatlin sighed with relief. *Idiot* was hardly a compliment, but it was a more comfortable fit than assassin. "She's hiring the world's most lethal killer, known only by his code name—the Ferret."

"So what's my job?"

"You're the go-between."

"Between...?"

"A rock and a hard place." She laughed. "Just teasing. But let's face it..." She looked around his shambolic quarters. "Even if it was true, would it matter? You've got everything to play for." She slid the money off the table and it dropped into his lap. "Real money and real hope. How long since you've had those? Besides, isn't it about time you joined the winning team?" Gatlin fondled the wad of bills. It was as if she'd read his thoughts. He nodded solemnly. "That's my boy."

"What do I have to do?"

"Con a few people into believing you're someone you're not."

"Like?"

"The Ferret's bag man."

Gatlin's eyes popped wide. "Pretend I work for a guy who's going to assassinate the president!" Now it was his turn to look around his shabby abode. It wasn't so bad, and it beat out a US penitentiary by a country mile.

"It's a fake assassination... it's not going to happen. Anyway, you'll be working indirectly for the president. If anything goes wrong, he'll pardon you like all the other crooks on his team. It's one of his qualities. He's real loyal like that."

"So who's this woman?"

The Witch fished out a phone and flashed a photo in front of him.

"Wow..."

"Yeah, Eve Coronata. She's a looker alright. She turned up out of nowhere on the beauty pageant circuit, then disappeared for years and reincarnated herself as a software billionaire."

"Out of nowhere?"

"No background, no family. Rumor is she was at a pageant sponsored by the big orange. They dated—I'm using the polite word here—and something went wrong."

"And she's still mad about it... after all this time?"

"He has a way of bringing out the best in a woman." The Witch eyed him speculatively as he ogled the photo. "So... are you in?"

"I don't know. Assassination. The US president. Even a fake one. What if it goes wrong and gets unfaked? He won't be around to pardon me."

"That's what the VP is for. And don't forget, you'll be the guy who got him the top job. He's going to love you."

Gatlin wobbled on the edge of commitment. Yes, he was desperate, but the downside... He stroked the money with his fingertips, a wistful look in his eyes. "And you do understand that this is just a retainer. I told you the whole thing's fake. So there's no assassin to pay. The money will be ours—yours and mine. We can split it fifty-fifty."

Gatlin's eyes flashed up at her, wistful no more. He seized the money with his left hand, slapped his right on his heart, and broke into song. *"Oh, say, can you see by the dawn's early light..."*

FOUR

Back in drama school, Felicity had learned an important lesson. Not in the classes, although all that acting stuff had come in handy during her various careers, but in the part-time job she'd worked to pay for them. Washing dishes had been a fast teacher, and she'd soon learned that not-washing-dishes was her preferred career path. She'd also learned that sometimes you have to do what you *don't want* to get what you *want*. And that pretty much summed up her relationship with Dimo.

Officially, he was her "influencer," meaning if she couldn't persuade Gatlin with her potent mix of intimidation and charm, he could bash the hapless Brit until he was influenced enough to reconsider. That was the *want* part of their relationship. The *don't want* part was the sex. Dimo was her new *washing-dishes*. Sex with the hired help had not been part of the plan, but it hadn't just happened either.

The trigger had been that wad of bills she'd been forking over on a daily basis to pay for his services. Euros might look like Monopoly money, but it had taken Felicity all of three milliseconds to figure out that they were for real. Besides, as a well-hung male with a ripped body and an exceedingly low IQ, Dimo had a lot to offer.

So, despite her predilection for portly gentlemen with fat wallets and bizarre fetishes, those attributes plus the crinkly bills had made the decision easy. Forty-eight hours after he'd picked her up at the airport, the deal was done. Not so much an arrangement as a head-over-heels love affair, albeit a fake one. And why not? Dimo wasn't married, and being an item meant sharing chores as in *you do that* and *I do this*, with anything risky or dangerous falling in Dimo's column and *taking care of the cash* ending up in Felicity's.

All that was good. The problem was the dreary, mechanical sex with him thumping back and forth like she was a rowing machine with only his dirty talk keeping her awake. *Eyin veh tri chaytiri* ... she had no idea what it meant, but she'd always enjoyed her sex with a running commentary, and his was inspirational, grunted out through gritted teeth. Real nasty.

As for the rest, the day-to-day grind of his company, his inane banter was an irritation she usually ignored. But as they drove back to their hotel in his mangy Euro sedan with shit AC, he told her about Benny's call, and she was still tuned in when he droned on, gloating about it all like he was now a blood brother of the boss.

"As I say to him, Benny, my friend, we will get them back... all our palaces."

"Palaces? You had palaces?"

"The Soviet communists steal them from my family. Now we go to EU court."

"You think you'll get them back?"

"For sure... but is small problem."

"How small?"

"EU court is located in our palace."

"Good luck with that, pal."

"Before communism was wonderful life. We own everything. Palaces... forests for hunting, rivers for fishing—"

"And peasants too. Don't forget them... the poor bastards eating dirt for breakfast."

"Phew... you make joke. It wasn't so bad. Sometimes they had milk with the dirt."

Felicity groaned and tuned out, turning her attention to the one useful snippet she'd gleaned from Dimo's report. Coronata was on her way. She reached for her phone and called Benny, letting it ring until it went to voicemail.

Benny's phone was on mute. Of course it was. He was under the sheets, watching the First Lady slide out of bed and slip on her silk robe. Crazy... but he envied that robe. Wasn't it enough that he'd just been there, his hands caressing her petal-soft skin, his whole being sliding between those endless thighs now swish-swashing towards the bathroom? Evidently, no. There was no *enough* where she was concerned, only more. He rolled on his side, propped his head up with his hand and peered at the bathroom door. She'd left it open. Just a tad.

Tempting.

When he heard the shower, he wanted to rush in and take her right there in a stream of heat and suds. But he sighed and slumped back on the pillow and stared at the ceiling instead.

In his dreams, maybe...

He'd swaggered naked into the bathroom during her toilette once before, and in the midst of a preliminary smooching session, she'd broken away, giggling.

"What?" he'd said, irritated, his stalky member already wilting.

She'd pointed to his image in the mirror.

"It's just so cute… your Humpty-Dumpty profile."

It was Benny's love moment from hell, now an image hard-coded on the inside of his skull, that his-and-hers look, its Halloween contrast, *hers* all linen-tan nakedness and photo-op features, *his* all ball-on-two-pencils goofiness. He'd never even noticed his ass before. He'd been sitting on it all his life and carrying it around everywhere without ever seeing it for what it was, vestigial, stunted by a lifetime of hard court benches, a modern American counterpart to the bound feet of Asia's lotus women in eons past. Simple fact—he had a lotus butt. Ever since that incident, he'd found creative ways of hiding it, becoming an expert at slipping out of his clothes and getting between the sheets with minimal flesh exposure.

He slid from under the covers, slipped on a gown and went through to the suite's living room, where he listened for the sound of the Secret Service beyond its double doors. He could make out their muffled voices, but not what they said. Everything sounded normal. He sat at the desk, where he'd arranged a pile of legal papers to make it look like he really was helping the First Lady with her charity work. Today's event in the hotel's ballroom was a fundraiser, and her scheduled appearance would allow those with too little money to get the ear of the president to at least get hers. He packed the papers away in his briefcase, then went back to the bedroom. He wanted a cigar like crazy, but she'd forbidden him from smoking and told him to dump that "filthy habit." Of course, he'd lied about that and told her he'd complied. He sat on the bed and checked his phone: one missed call.

Felicity.

An update from Europe. He glanced at the bathroom door. Ina's showers were forever events, but he'd still better make this quick.

"Is Fry hooked?" he said as soon as he heard her voice.

"Line and sinker. Is the meet all set?"

"Coronata is sending her Turk."

"With the money."

"Partial payment. That'll be your working cash from here on out. Use it to pay Brainiac."

"Yeah, I heard you spoke to my little Dimmy."

"You never told me you had royalty on your team."

"Is he full of it or what?"

"But will he do?"

"He's got wheels and muscles. That's all I need him for."

"We'll fix the final payment for Paris. Just before the big event."

"Got it."

"Did you check that Ferret stuff I sent you?"

"Done already."

He noticed the First Lady standing in the bathroom doorway, brushing her hair, and hung up.

"The Ferret stuff?" she said.

He waved his hand at the phone dismissively like it was nothing worth talking about.

"You wouldn't believe it anyway."

"Try me."

She put the brush on the nightstand and sat on the bed next to him.

"Horndog's latest stunt... a fake assassination."

"Why fake?" They shared a chuckle, a cheater's joke. "Let me guess. Boost his ratings?"

"Not only that. There's some old flame from—"

The end of his sentence got wiped clean by the look on her face.

"Go on…"

The president's extramarital affairs were hardly news to his wife. But even so, this was swampy ground.

"One of the contestants from that Moscow pageant is looking for an assassin."

"Code name the Ferret?"

"You really don't want to know."

She nodded. "You're right. But I can send her my best wishes." She stood up and crossed herself, raising her eyes to heaven. "Good luck, madam." She checked her watch. "My makeup crew will be here in ten minutes. So…" She jerked her thumb at the door. Benny left her to her preparations. He threw on his clothes, grabbed his briefcase and left. An hour later, he was on his way back to Manhattan, sitting alone in the corporate jet and thinking hard.

The Ferret stuff…

Too bad the First Lady had heard that. And in the dewy afterglow of love, he'd been dumb enough to tell her the truth, not that a plausible explanation of the term was an easy reach. Little things count. That was Benny's takeaway from all those years as a prosecutor. Things overheard got repeated, and often had consequences like a lifetime in jail. He looked out the window. He could just make out the shimmer of the Atlantic Ocean on the horizon. She'd probably forget it. It was a busy day for her, only a short speech to give, but then she had a hundred hands to shake. She'd never…

He stopped. Who was he kidding? Never remember? Some old flame looking for an assassin! She'd never *forget* was the truth of it. Benny closed his eyes and eased his head back onto the seat, knowing with a certainty that today was a day he was sure to regret.

Somewhere between Paris and Alicante, Zaza was sky high too. He was staring out the jet's window, equally lost in his thoughts. He'd ducked the decision and avoided giving her a hard yes or no, but... He peered down at the landscape below. Farms and villages had given way to mountains, not pretty pointy ones, but lusty weathered stumps that looked as old as time. The Pyrenees? Most likely. That meant they'd be landing soon. He'd have to stop wobbling and tell her one way or another.

"Maybe if I understood why. Is it a political thing?"

"I don't give a damn about his politics."

"Then what?" Now it was Eve's turn to look out the window. They were sitting in leather wingback chairs on opposite sides of the aisle. "Something personal?"

"I can't talk about it."

"You met him?"

"Met?" She barked it out, suddenly aggressive. "Does that have some special meaning in the Koran like *know* in the Bible? *Adam knew Eve, his wife; and she conceived.* Well... we met, but then again... we didn't *meet.*"

"When was this?"

"At that notorious Miss Universe in Russia."

Notorious?

Zaza had no idea why. He'd read a few tabloid headlines about the John Thomas, scandals involving women. Then there'd been that audio tape—the US President extolling the perks of fame, delighting in his pussy grabbing exploits. The whole world had enjoyed that one.

"So what happ—"

She put up her hand like a traffic cop. "It's totally personal."

Zaza quit that line of inquiry, although not his interest in it. That doubled every time she shut him down.

"So I don't need to pull the trigger?"

"I guarantee it."

"How did you find the Ferret?"

"I spent years tracking him and a month or so ago, I found him. Now I have to make a payment. Good faith money to get it started."

"What if it's a con?"

"It can't be. I had inside information about the Ferret's previous killings. I tested him. It must be him."

"Maybe he is a cop and it's a trap."

"It's possible, but not likely. It took me forever to find him. Who makes a trap so well hidden it can almost never be found?"

"And all I have to do is hand over some cash?"

"And negotiate terms. It'll be easy. I'll give you a scanner. You can make sure you're not being recorded."

"You seem to have it all worked out. But what if it goes wrong and you lose your money?"

"I'll pay every cent I own to hang that yellow scalp on my wall. So what's your real answer? Can we trade dreams?"

Zaza nodded. "I'll meet with the guy. I'll make the payment."

She put her hand on her heart and he could read the relief on her face. He'd done the right thing. He couldn't let her handle this alone, a woman delivering cash to an assassin's accomplice, or some crooked con man. No way was he going to let her face that alone. Besides, it was most likely a con, and even if it wasn't, there'd be ways to bail out or sabotage it down the road. He looked out the window at the sea on the horizon, the Mediterranean, stretching all the way to Bodrum, and for a moment, his eyes folded time and space. He could see it all—the villa, the yacht, the lifestyle. But where was Beverly? Nowhere to be seen. Holding his arm as they sauntered along the marina was his beautiful butterfly boss.

FIVE

The Money.

It was still there the next day when Gatlin emerged from a fourteen-hour cannabis-modulated hibernation.

The phone.

That was still there too.

It wasn't a dream.

Gatlin's mind raced back over recent events. The pot heist, his curt dismissal by the brownshirt Brunhilda, the windy dawn and the rat-dog-branch miracle on the bench—it all made sense now. He'd called to God and his prayers had been answered. Pretty shocking, that. Not only that God had listened, but that Gatlin had made the request. Keeping in step with the British government, he didn't do God in the normal way of things, his cosmic vision, like theirs, being more karma-oriented and distilled into a one-word theology known as payback. By his reckoning, he was due. He was overdue. And here was the delivery, filthy lucre served by a goddess, a yummilicious witch with a remote-control vagina jacked into his brain. If ever there was a cause for celebration, this was it. He reached for his bong.

But then again...

He set it aside, surprising himself, and sucked a few breaths through the nose instead, flaring his nostrils yoga style, energizing his ethereal body, or some such shit.

Bong, booze... don't need it.

Yes, sir, this was the new Gatlin, cleansed and reborn. He couldn't afford to blunt his razor-sharp reflexes with dope, to dull his agile mind with booze. Instructions from the Witch were imminent. He fiddled with his new phone to pass the time, then counted the euro bills until hunger rumbled in his belly. He peeled off a few notes and pocketed them, then stuffed his wad in his fanny pack along with the phone.

It was sunny and warm outside, and he stood for a moment, enjoying its warmth, looking up at the sun with his eyes closed, pumping up his vitamin D. Suitably fortified, although missing mightily his breakfast bong, Gatlin strode towards the exit and stopped at the office by the gate, a thought pulling him up sharp. What if the Witch of Langley was not who she made herself out to be? This moment of doubt shocked him. If she wasn't, why would she give him money? Gatlin racked his brains but could come up with no answer. She knew about his background with MI6? Who else but a CIA agent would know that? Even so—crazy as it was—he couldn't get the notion out of his head. This kind of giddy good luck he was having was so un-Gatlinish.

He trotted into the campsite office, where the manager was plucking at a keyboard with the rhythm of someone getting paid per hour and not per key. Lieke was in her fifties with what Gatlin thought of as a peasant's build, meaning she was thickset and looked well able to wrestle large bovines. She glanced up at him expressionless, her florid face crusty with sunburn and so round it reminded him of an Edam cheese.

"Money," she said, her eyes going back to her keyboard plunking. "Or next Friday, you're out on your arse." Gatlin stood in front of her on the customer side of the counter, but she didn't look up. He could have shown her the money then, but he let her drone on, peppering her threats with plenty of throaty Dutch sounds like she was about to hawk up a gooey mouthful. He waited until she got to the *forcible eviction* part before sprinkling fifty-euro bills down on her keyboard. She stopped typing but still didn't look up, her eyes never leaving the money.

"I thought I'd pay the next couple of months in advance, if that's no inconvenience. I have some travel planned, some business in the States to attend to."

He waited while she collected the money and counted it.

"Receipt?" she said.

"That's okay. I trust you." He went to go but turned back as if getting caught by an afterthought. "My neighbor tells me I had some visitors yesterday while I was out. They didn't leave a message. So could I take a quick look at your camera feed to see who it was?" He pointed at the bank of black-and-white monitors on the wall behind her. "The one on the parking lot should do it." She locked the money inside a metal box in a drawer under the counter.

"No."

Gatlin nodded. It was to be expected. He was far from a model tenant, and the year before he'd spent a boozy night with Lieke and he'd ended up in her bed, where, allegedly, he'd made certain promises that had not survived the dawn.

"Still mad at me, eh?"

"Fuck off."

Gatlin left. Hard to negotiate with such a plain-speaking woman. He walked around the office building to a fenced-off recycling area, its metal dumpsters keyed in different colors for different types of waste. Carton and paper should do. He whipped out his Zippo, and by the time he was back in the office, a good blaze was underway.

"Are you burning the rubbish now instead of recycling it?" he said.

"What?"

"There are cinders blowing all over the place." He whipped out his phone. "Should I call the *bomberos*?" She leapt up, grabbed a fire extinguisher and ran out of the office.

Gatlin knew he didn't have long. It wasn't much of a fire and she'd have it doused in seconds. He slipped behind the desk and fiddled at her keyboard. She'd been in too much of a hurry to log off. He found the parking lot camera and rewound the recording, guided by the on-screen time stamp, and soon found...

Skoda!

She's driving a Skoda?

Gatlin took a couple of shots of the screen with his phone. The Czech auto had a male driver who'd hurried to get the passenger door for her, a real gent with wide shoulders and a narrow waist to go with his good manners.

Gatlin was on his way out when he passed Lieke coming the other way. She was still toting the extinguisher and her face was smudged with black residue from her battle with the flames. She glared at him as he waved and bade his farewell.

He headed to his favorite greasy-spoon diner, where he was shoveling a full-English into his belly when his new phone rang...

The Witch.

He listened to her instructions as he dipped his bacon in egg yolk and forked it home, chewing thoughtfully. He had to meet a man and play the Ferret's fixer. She sent him the man's photo: big and round with a smiley face. If he'd been called Mr. Emoji, it would have been perfect, but Gatlin was told to address him as Mr. Z. He could do all that. Cloak-and-dagger stuff. Just like the good old days. He went back to his food, and it was only when he'd finished eating and was supping more tea that he remembered the snap he'd taken from the CCTV feed. He wanted to get a closer look at the car and driver. He took out his phone and pulled up the photo, noticing something strange about that Skoda right away. How could he have missed it? The registration plate was weird—he zoomed in on it—and the country code was BG instead of ES for España. BG? He stuck it in a search engine...

Strange... I didn't even know the CIA had a Bulgarian branch.

As Gatlin pondered the implications of his discovery, an ocean away, Benny watched the First Lady sign the last of the papers, a video recorder in his head catching every nuance of her. Those long fingers, her pale pink nails tipped with white, the rings, the unmissable rings, all nine million dollars' worth—no detail escaped his loving gaze. When she'd finished, she slid the top back on the pen, laid it down, and locked eyes with him in silence while the notary signed each document. This was the end of their charity project work together; the excuse that had cloaked their affair was about to be stripped off. So where to from here? The First Lady could hardly make an excuse like *popping out to the corner store* to cover their assignations.

After the notary had left, she was the first to speak.

"Are they actually going to shoot him?" she said, opening a topic way off base and catching him wrong-footed.

He looked around nervously.

This is my goddamn office.

Not that it mattered. He had it swept for bugs on a weekly basis.

"He's not that stupid."

She kept him nailed with that inscrutable stare, her disappointment writ large on her chiseled features.

"So what, then?"

"We set up a fake Ferret trail and Coronata—that's the woman—is about to fall into the hole we dug on it by making the first of two payments. When she makes the second—or her man does—the FBI will be waiting with a bunch of French cops."

"Reagan was shot. Thatcher was bombed. It's not the same."

"No, but he'll get a bounce, and nothing she ever says about him will be believed."

"Poor woman... you should be ashamed for helping him."

"She wants to kill your husband."

"I know the feeling." She paced in front of his desk, her arms crossed. He left her to it. This conversation was headed nowhere, and he needed to track it back on something more meaningful, like *what's next for us?*

She stopped abruptly and swirled to face him. "What if there was a real Ferret?"

"I don't get it. I'm the Ferret... the fake Ferret. I give the orders."

"What if you contacted the real Ferret, or some other assassin? Horndog is stumping up the money himself. So you've already got the cash. It's the perfect murder. My dumb husband has set it all up for us. You're the puppet master. So pull the right strings. That file on the Ferret, doesn't it give you any idea how to—"

"Stop... forget it. This conversation never happened."

She snatched up her bag off his desk.

"Agreed. Let's forget it. Let's forget the whole damn thing." She offered him her hand. "Thank you, Mr. Capone, for your pro bono work on my charitable endeavors. I'll let the president know what a great help you've been. Give my regards to Mrs. Capone."

His eyes went back and forth from the hand still waiting for attention and her impassive face. No way to win this one. He shook her hand somberly—"Madame First Lady"—and watched her leave, his face puckering and his spirit tumbling.

When darkness came, Benny was still sitting behind his desk in his big leather chair. The staff had gone home already, but still he waited, staring at the puddle of light from the desk lamp.

What if?

Her words kept playing over and over. He did know guys. Of course he did. He'd been a prosecutor, his dad a mobster. But he wasn't his dad. That was the whole point of his life. He was a lawyer. He fiddled with his computer to pass the time, pulling up the Ferret dossier. He'd hardly read it. Just enough to give Felicity a script to play out. There was something he remembered, though, a Swiss lawyer who'd been under suspicion as a contact for the Ferret. His phone buzzed, a message with no contact name, but he recognized the number. Ina's burner phone. The one he'd given her. He reached for it but jerked his hand back at the last minute.

What was he expecting, an apology… a love note?

She wasn't the type.

It had to be the coup de grâce. The "kiss-off, loser" farewell note. He couldn't face that right now. He unlocked his wall safe and took out a sixty-year-old scotch. He poured a good measure, about five thousand dollars' worth, into a glass and chugged it back. Then he poured another, replaced the bottle in the safe and returned to his desk, where his eyes wandered back to the computer. Arnold Buhlmann-Fischer. That was the suspect's name, an attorney of noted ill repute even for a Swiss lawyer. The investigation had never gone anywhere due to jurisdictional this and that and no doubt a bundle of Swiss francs stuck under the Christmas tree of some Swiss prosecutor.

His phone rang. He wasn't in the mood, but he had to check it. That was the pain of working for…

Rump.

He grabbed the phone. "Sir…"

"Hey, Benny, what's up?"

"Just winding down, sir. It was a long day."

"Yeah, so I heard. Finishing up with my wife."

Benny's backbone snapped straight so fast his new toupee nearly hit the wall.

"Oh… the… em… charity… yes, so glad to help, sir."

"Say, Benny, do you remember that CNN interview where you said *I'd take a bullet for the president?*"

"Never forget it. I couldn't let those bastards beat up on you like that, sir."

"So... is that still true?"

Benny was getting a strange feeling about this conversation... all that talk about bullets.

"Damn right it is. Anytime, anywhere."

"That's great. So where are you now?"

Yeah... definitely, this is a weird conversation.

"The office, sir, burning the midnight—"

"Do me a favor. Stay there. I'm sending a man with a gun, so you can prove it... you lying, cheating *wop*."

Benny remained motionless, comforted by the sudden dial tone, its familiarity, its ordinariness. Then he stared at the phone before dropping it, and as it clattered on the desk, he noticed its blinking LED... the First Lady's message. He snatched it up.

He caught me crying. I had to tell him the truth. He's never seen me cry before, so he wanted to send me to the hospital. Good luck in Normandy. If it all goes well... so many ifs. Could it be? Humpty and me. Am I just a crazy dreamer...? xxx

Benny dropped the phone again, although not intentionally. It just flew out of his hand when it started shaking, his whole body bouncing around like a finalist in a dad dancing contest. He ran out of his private office and through reception to the door to his suite.

Locked.

He jammed a chair under the handle but then felt really stupid about that.

A chair?

He's sending SEAL Team Six, you asshole!

No, wait. He couldn't do that. This was the United States, not Belarus. That said, Rump was a big fan of the Belarussian president, calling his bestseller, *High-Caliber Votes: Elections Made Easy*, a guidebook of biblical awesomeness. But if not special forces, then what? He went to the window and scanned the skies... *a drone?* No, that was ridiculous. Rump owned real estate in Manhattan and there was nothing like a Hellfire missile to crash property prices. He'd hire a private killer like the Ferret, only a lot cheaper, and negotiate a two-for-one deal, or at least a discount for knocking off his wife at the same time. Most likely, it'd be a sniper who... *aargh*...

He leapt back from the window and dropped to the floor.

Idiot.

He could be up there already, sitting on a rooftop opposite and fiddling with his scope. Benny crawled back into his private office and dropped the blinds, then tiptoed to his desk and flopped into its chair.

No... it wouldn't happen in his office. It would be later when he'd least expect it. He'd be having a massage at a spa and someone would come in. He'd look up and slip his glasses on to see who it was and— *bam*, get it straight through the glass and into his eyeball like what's-his-name in what's-that-movie. He slugged back the scotch. How could she have been so stupid as to tell him? What woas she thinking? He read her message again. *Good luck in Normandy*? What was that all about? He wasn't even going to France, and... *Humpty and me.* That was all he needed right now, a recap of his love moment from hell. As for *crazy dreamer*, the crazy part was right on the money, she—

He broke off with the message decoding in his head in flashing neon...

DO IT! KILL MY HUSBAND.

Crazy? Maybe.

Calculating? Absolutely.

Now it all made sense: his unceremonious dumping, but only after she'd laid out her perfect-murder plan. Then tears for the president. An Oscar-winning performance, no doubt. And to follow up, a gesture, a wafting finger, a message to say *if only*. He went to the safe and poured another scotch.

He's under my thumb... that's what she figures.

He gulped his drink, not tasting it, but feeling it, his heart pounding.

I'll show her... I'm going to—

What?

He had no plan now. So he went back to the message...

Humpty and me.

The words were a time machine taking him back to that day, that bathroom. Two naked lovers. He'd read that all wrong. She hadn't meant it as a put-down. *Humpty and me...* it was kind of cute. He rolled it over and over under his breath, still trapped in that bathroom, his hands on her petal-soft skin, caressing those exquisitely engineered breasts and wallowing between her perfect thighs—

The fake Ferret sting?

What was to become of it? The Very Stable Genius in the White House had obviously forgotten about it.

Arnold Buhlmann-Fischer...

Benny stared at the name on the computer screen and sipped his scotch. So what if he were to make an exploratory call, a personal outreach, shyster to shyster? It just might work. Ina was right. It was all set up. All he had to do was connect the dots. With Horndog dead, he'd be *the man*. She'd be in his pocket. Publishers would bid like crazy for his book, working title *Rump and Circumstance*. He'd comfort the bereaved widow and be her judicial knight, filing lawsuits against Rump's scumbag kids fighting for their fair share and whining about her prenup. He checked the world clock for the local time in Zug. He'd have to wait hours. But so what? He was stuck in the office anyway. He picked up his phone to order food delivery.

Risky... better make it Italian.

Benny knew people he could trust... well, *Italian trust*, so best avoid the pizza. Something in boxes too small to hide a gun would be perfect.

Following through on that wisdom, dinner was delivered without incident, and that was followed by coffee, cigars and yet more whiskey to keep him pumped way through the night.

When it finally came, their conversation was long and circuitous and set to the soundtrack of two rattlesnakes fornicating. But when dawn broke, the deal was done. Assassination, or any synonym thereof, was a word never uttered or implied. Nothing close. It was merely an introduction, a reference. No papers. No trail to audit, and just one clue. Coronata had used the nym Sea Urchin in her online quest, and Benny made it the password, the certificate of authenticity, tying her to the real Ferret. It was a small point, and evidentially, merely circumstantial. But Benny knew how to frame suspects, and how juries ticked, and little things like this made big things happen. As for the rest, their chat was lawyerly with plenty of does-your-back-itch innuendo. There was talk of a donation to an obscure charity with an odd preference for crypto, and in due course a referral was provided, an address on the dark web, a black hole where messages appeared and disappeared almost as quickly. The rest was up to Benny.

SIX

The gap between expectation and reality gagged Gatlin into silence. The Witch's photo was a portrait of a man with a face rounded out by muscular jowls, its features laid out with trigonometric precision under a thatch of thinning black tufts, its smile sunny-looking, warm and friendly.

So who's this?

The face was still round, but it wasn't smiling, or warm and friendly. It was dark and foreboding, coated with black stubble, jaw muscles bulging like a pit bull, black eyes knitted together by finger-thick eyebrows. Then there was the body. With only the face to work with, Gatlin had filled in the blanks—a big man for sure, but gone to seed, the sort of man you see propping up a bar and balancing a pint on his belly as he spins a jovial yarn, a round man to match that round face. But this man was square, his torso almost as wide as it was long. *Think... refrigerator.* And not one of those wimpy Euro jobs either, but an American fridge with a freezer, icemaker, water-cooler and enough space left over to park several midsize sedans.

This was the reality of the man who towered over Gatlin, offering his hand.

"Mr. G?"

"Sir..." Gatlin wobbled up onto his feet. He'd skipped his breakfast bong again, part of his new keep-fit regimen, and he was regretting it, his perspective skewed in a down-the-rabbit-hole sort of way that had him wondering if this man really was that big or if his bigness was merely a hallucinogenic brainfart.

"Mr. Z." He shook the proffered hand with both of his own, a body-language signal conveying warmth, honesty and trust. Although in Gatlin's case, he just needed both hands to accommodate Z's massive paw.

They were meeting on the promenade at Benidorm's Levante beach, a public spot by design, its approach festooned with cameras, its sands streaming live to the world on umpteen webcams. Z took his seat across from Gatlin at one of the public chess tables there. To those cameras, or to any passerby, they might have been two acquaintances meeting for a quick game, or equally well, two strangers, two lonely men passing time together.

"Are you wearing a wire?" Z said as soon as they were seated.

Gatlin didn't answer, his reflex to lie stalled by a street-dog instinct.

Sniff, sniff...

Opportunity!

He was indeed recording the session, or rather the Witch was via the phone she'd given him. Gatlin plugged the moment into his needs-goals axis—the one that ran from American teeth to a genuine Winnebago—and hit a red-hot wire.

If I had no option but to shut down the phone, I'd be free to write my own script.

Z took out a gizmo and aimed it at him, obviously some sort of scanner.

"No need for that scanner," Gatlin said, loud enough for his phone mic to pick it up. "I'll turn off my phone if you turn off yours."

Z nodded, and they both made a show of shutting down their phones.

"So?" Gatlin said when both phones were tucked out of sight, "where's the upfront?"

Z took a newspaper out of a briefcase and laid it on the table by the chessboard, but he kept his hairy mitt on it. "Terms, time and place... we need to talk first. If I like what I hear, you take the newspaper when you leave."

"Okay."

"Shall we?" He waved at the chessboard. "For appearance's sake." He didn't wait for an answer, plucking two pieces off the board, one black and one white, and holding his balled fists outstretched. His movements were slow, not threatening, but those scarred knuckles squeezed between wads of muscle made Gatlin gulp. Gatlin pointed at the right hand and Mr. Z revealed a black piece. He then replaced both pieces and led with white.

Gatlin studied the board like he knew what he was doing, then moved a piece, one of the dorky little ones in the front row.

"That's an illegal move," Mr. Z said. "Pawns don't go diagonally."

"I'm a bit rusty." Gatlin made the adjustment, placing the piece so it exactly mirrored his opponent's move. "How about that?" He wiped the sweat from his brow onto his sleeve. All the shaded tables had been taken by the time he'd arrived, so this baker's oven spot was the best he could do. Now he'd been sitting here for an hour and the midday sun was threatening his overheated brain with a meltdown. This stupid chess game wasn't helping either. That had been the

Witch's idea, and now he regretted his prideful *of course I can play*, but she'd been so snooty about it.

"Can't we just do the deal?" he said.

"Why not talk as we play? It'll look more natural."

Gatlin wanted to argue the point. But the newspaper was on the table, the money tantalizingly close. All he had to do was play along, swallow his pride and make nice. Too bad he couldn't play chess too.

"I haven't sat behind a chessboard for years," Z continued. "I loved the game as a kid, planned to be a grandmaster... make a career of it."

"So what happened?"

"I took up oil wrestling instead."

Gatlin considered that, but despite his considerable imagination, he could make no sense of it. "So how's that work, then?"

"Excuse me."

"Wrestling oil?" Z didn't answer, but he did blink. Over and over. "For example... how d'you do a forearm lock on it?" Big man or no, Gatlin wasn't in the mood for bullshit like this. *No one wrestles oil. It's too slippery for starters.*

Z sat back, his puzzled scowl diminishing into a worried parent look.

"Maybe you're right. Let's just hash out the terms, make a few moves and be on our way." He moved a pawn. "The president is scheduled to visit France for the D-Day commemorations in June. That will present an ideal opportunity."

"What about the final payment?"

"Up to one million. Come back to me with terms. We'll need confirmation of the time frame first. The final payment can be made a few days before. In Paris, for example." He waved at the board. "Your move."

One million?

Gatlin stared at the board, struggling to keep a poker face.

One million what?

It didn't matter. Anything would do. Stuff the Winnebago. With money like that, he could get a customized Hollywood RV like—

Stay cool.

"Yeah..." He moved a pawn forward two squares, avoiding the diagonal faux pas he'd made earlier, adding with quiet confidence, "this is all coming back now... like riding a bike."

Z countermoved, taking Gatlin's pawn with one of his own and placing it on the table next to the board.

"Hey... you said no diagonal moves."

"That's when you *move*. This is *taking*. Pawns move vertically, but they take diagonally."

That had to be pure crap. The Russians invented chess. They were smart people. They wouldn't make a stupid rule like that. Gatlin fumed in silence with some arcane law of psycho-physics pumping up his brain pressure. The mathematics of it were simple. Add one hour of sitting in the egg-fry Spanish sun to the square of his cannabis cold turkey, then multiply the result by how pissed off he was with this chess malarkey, and leave Z to add the backbreaking straw...

"You've got no idea how to play this game, have you?"

No idea, no idea...

Gatlin let the insult ricochet back and forth inside his skull for long enough to mash his gray matter into goo, then said, "Are you an Arab?" thrusting his head out on his stringy neck, inadvertently replicating

Brunhilda's throttled turkey-penis image from scene one.

"What's it to you?"

"You look foreign… and your play here. They're Arab rules. I was playing English chess. Different rules. You see this big one here with the knobbly top?" He picked up his king. "In English rules you can do this…" He leaned across the board and bashed each of his opponent's pieces one by one. Z watched impassively as pieces rolled into his lap and others hit the floor. "There…" Gatlin placed his king at the center of the board. "Checkmate, I believe that's the term." He smirked, arms crossed. But his moment of triumph lasted only as long as it took him to register Z's face. No longer round and avuncular, now square and Neanderthal, those massive jaw muscles set like broken bricks, his head thrust forward to match Gatlin's, his thick neck not so much turkey-penis as Spanish fighting bull.

Gatlin shriveled back in his seat, stunned by his own madness

Why?

He posed the question but had no answer. He'd gone berserk for reason or reasons unknown, and now his wanna-have future, the American-teeth dream, was about to be replaced by the don't-wanna-have nightmare of him crawling back to his hovel with no teeth at all. Then there'd be the aftermath, the reckoning with the Witch, her beefy driver pinning him to a wall while she gutted him with her titanium nails.

And why?

Because he'd thrown a hissy fit.

The bong.

Or rather, the no-bong. It was the only explanation that made sense. That morning smoke had been an integral part of his breakfast-of-champions for years and skipping it had been a dumb move. He'd played it by the book for once. He'd done the right thing. He'd abstained. And this situation—the glowering refrigerator pulsating in front of him—was the direct consequence. That morning toke was essential medication, a THC anchor stabilizing his brain. And today of all days, he'd skipped it. He'd cut the chain and now he was about to crash on the rocks.

Desperate measures were called for...

"Only kidding, mate." He held out his hand for the shake. "I wanted it to look like we were having fun, so no one would ever believe there was anything serious going down."

Z looked at the hand, and Gatlin was expecting one of those big fists to crash into him at any moment. But Z surprised him, uncurling his fists and shaking his hand, a quick shake to be sure, but enough to encourage Gatlin to reach for the newspaper. Z grabbed his wrist just as he touched it, and pain arced up his arm and slammed into his eyeballs. Z didn't so much as squeeze his wrist as roll the bones, crunching and grinding them together as he pulled Gatlin in close.

"I was crowned *baspehlivan*—champion wrestler— at the Kırkpınar, Turkey's annual oil wrestling tournament and the world's oldest sporting event. We don't wrestle oil, *moron*. Combatants cover themselves with olive oil and fight. The object is to grab your opponent and heave him to the ground. Do you have any idea how hard it is to throw a greased-up Turk on his back, especially a fat one wearing only leather undies?"

Gatlin hit information overload: *greased up... leather undies...* that was way too much detail for him. Z loosened his grip and leaned his ear in closer to catch Gatlin's squeaky response, "Only guessing... very hard."

"So you know how easy it would be for me to hurl an ungreased Brit, a puny one with a marshmallow belly and convenient handles on his head, right up on to that roof there." He nodded to a nearby building. It was a ridiculous exaggeration, and in the normal way of things Gatlin would have been stupid enough to call him out on it, maybe even bet him he couldn't and place a wager to back it up. But in view of Z's bone-crunching exhibition, he kept shtum. Suddenly, Z smiled and let him go. It was such an about-face it caught Gatlin on the hop with no idea what to make of it. He rubbed his sore wrist and whimpered.

"What's your real name?" Z said. "Mine's Zaza."

"Gatlin."

"I like you, Gatlin, in a perverse sort of way—"

"I'm not a pervert," Gatlin was quick to note, that image of greased-up Turks rolling around in the dirt a sudden and unwelcome flashback.

"I just mean... it's okay if you're crazy. I spent fifteen years of my life oiling my body up like a shrimp on a barbecue and fighting monstrously savage men. Why? There was no money in it. No global TV audience like football, and oil wrestlers don't get Nike sponsorships either. You'd think the olive oil companies would line up. But they showed me the door. Apparently greasy fat boys slapping each other around is not a *brand enhancer*. So why did I do it? Glory. If that's not crazy, then what is?" Gatlin was relieved to have moved on, but it felt like they'd navigated from a swamp to a quicksand. What explained this sudden gear shift? Why was he being nice to him after grinding his bones? Zaza picked up the newspaper and handed it to him, and Gatlin took it like a wary dog sneaking a scrap of food.

"One last thing... on page two of the newspaper, there is a three-word note, the name of a secure messaging app, a username, and a password. All communication must occur through that channel and only between you and me. This is a nonnegotiable requirement. My principal insists on it. The link goes from her to me and from you to the Ferret. Agreed?"

Gatlin was ecstatic, pain forgotten. Zaza, his new best friend, had just cut the Witch out of the deal.

"That is acceptable," he said, stifling the word *Whoopee!*

"Are you sure you're comfortable with all that stuff? Downloading the app, for example—you're not *rusty* on *downloading*, are you?"

"No, sir. Totally up to speed on the whole loading skill set... uploading, downloading, getting loaded. It's all second nature to me."

Z chuckled artfully. "In that case, go with God, my friend. We'll be in touch."

SEVEN

The gap between expectation and reality gagged Gatlin into silence. The Witch's photo was a portrait of a man with a face rounded out by muscular jowls, its features laid out with trigonometric precision under a thatch of thinning black tufts, its smile sunny-looking, warm and friendly.

So who's this?

The face was still round, but it wasn't smiling, or warm and friendly. It was dark and foreboding, coated with black stubble, jaw muscles bulging like a pit bull, black eyes knitted together by finger-thick eyebrows. Then there was the body. With only the face to work with, Gatlin had filled in the blanks—a big man for sure, but gone to seed, the sort of man you see propping up a bar and balancing a pint on his belly as he spins a jovial yarn, a round man to match that round face. But this man was square, his torso almost as wide as it was long. *Think... refrigerator*. And not one of those wimpy Euro jobs either, but an American fridge with a freezer, icemaker, water-cooler and enough space left over to park several midsize sedans.

This was the reality of the man who towered over Gatlin, offering his hand.

"Mr. G?"

"Sir..." Gatlin wobbled up onto his feet. He'd skipped his breakfast bong again, part of his new keep-fit regimen, and he was regretting it, his perspective skewed in a down-the-rabbit-hole sort of way that had him wondering if this man really was that big or if his bigness was merely a hallucinogenic brainfart.

"Mr. Z." He shook the proffered hand with both of his own, a body-language signal conveying warmth, honesty and trust. Although in Gatlin's case, he just needed both hands to accommodate Z's massive paw.

They were meeting on the promenade at Benidorm's Levante beach, a public spot by design, its approach festooned with cameras, its sands streaming live to the world on umpteen webcams. Z took his seat across from Gatlin at one of the public chess tables there. To those cameras, or to any passerby, they might have been two acquaintances meeting for a quick game, or equally well, two strangers, two lonely men passing time together.

"Are you wearing a wire?" Z said as soon as they were seated.

Gatlin didn't answer, his reflex to lie stalled by a street-dog instinct.

Sniff, sniff...

Opportunity!

He was indeed recording the session, or rather the Witch was via the phone she'd given him. Gatlin plugged the moment into his needs-goals axis—the one that ran from American teeth to a genuine Winnebago—and hit a red-hot wire.

If I had no option but to shut down the phone, I'd be free to write my own script.

Z took out a gizmo and aimed it at him, obviously some sort of scanner.

"No need for that scanner," Gatlin said, loud enough for his phone mic to pick it up. "I'll turn off my phone if you turn off yours."

Z nodded, and they both made a show of shutting down their phones.

"So?" Gatlin said when both phones were tucked out of sight, "where's the upfront?"

Z took a newspaper out of a briefcase and laid it on the table by the chessboard, but he kept his hairy mitt on it. "Terms, time and place... we need to talk first. If I like what I hear, you take the newspaper when you leave."

"Okay."

"Shall we?" He waved at the chessboard. "For appearance's sake." He didn't wait for an answer, plucking two pieces off the board, one black and one white, and holding his balled fists outstretched. His movements were slow, not threatening, but those scarred knuckles squeezed between wads of muscle made Gatlin gulp. Gatlin pointed at the right hand and Mr. Z revealed a black piece. He then replaced both pieces and led with white.

Gatlin studied the board like he knew what he was doing, then moved a piece, one of the dorky little ones in the front row.

"That's an illegal move," Mr. Z said. "Pawns don't go diagonally."

"I'm a bit rusty." Gatlin made the adjustment, placing the piece so it exactly mirrored his opponent's move. "How about that?" He wiped the sweat from his brow onto his sleeve. All the shaded tables had been taken by the time he'd arrived, so this baker's oven spot was the best he could do. Now he'd been sitting here for an hour and the midday sun was threatening his overheated brain with a meltdown. This stupid chess game wasn't helping either. That had been the

Witch's idea, and now he regretted his prideful *of course I can play*, but she'd been so snooty about it.

"Can't we just do the deal?" he said.

"Why not talk as we play? It'll look more natural."

Gatlin wanted to argue the point. But the newspaper was on the table, the money tantalizingly close. All he had to do was play along, swallow his pride and make nice. Too bad he couldn't play chess too.

"I haven't sat behind a chessboard for years," Z continued. "I loved the game as a kid, planned to be a grandmaster... make a career of it."

"So what happened?"

"I took up oil wrestling instead."

Gatlin considered that, but despite his considerable imagination, he could make no sense of it. "So how's that work, then?"

"Excuse me."

"Wrestling oil?" Z didn't answer, but he did blink. Over and over. "For example... how d'you do a forearm lock on it?" Big man or no, Gatlin wasn't in the mood for bullshit like this. *No one wrestles oil. It's too slippery for starters.*

Z sat back, his puzzled scowl diminishing into a worried parent look.

"Maybe you're right. Let's just hash out the terms, make a few moves and be on our way." He moved a pawn. "The president is scheduled to visit France for the D-Day commemorations in June. That will present an ideal opportunity."

"What about the final payment?"

"Up to one million. Come back to me with terms. We'll need confirmation of the time frame first. The final payment can be made a few days before. In Paris, for example." He waved at the board. "Your move."

One million?

Gatlin stared at the board, struggling to keep a poker face.

One million what?

It didn't matter. Anything would do. Stuff the Winnebago. With money like that, he could get a customized Hollywood RV like—

Stay cool.

"Yeah…" He moved a pawn forward two squares, avoiding the diagonal faux pas he'd made earlier, adding with quiet confidence, "this is all coming back now… like riding a bike."

Z countermoved, taking Gatlin's pawn with one of his own and placing it on the table next to the board.

"Hey… you said no diagonal moves."

"That's when you *move*. This is *taking*. Pawns move vertically, but they take diagonally."

That had to be pure crap. The Russians invented chess. They were smart people. They wouldn't make a stupid rule like that. Gatlin fumed in silence with some arcane law of psycho-physics pumping up his brain pressure. The mathematics of it were simple. Add one hour of sitting in the egg-fry Spanish sun to the square of his cannabis cold turkey, then multiply the result by how pissed off he was with this chess malarkey, and leave Z to add the backbreaking straw…

"You've got no idea how to play this game, have you?"

No idea, no idea…

Gatlin let the insult ricochet back and forth inside his skull for long enough to mash his gray matter into goo, then said, "Are you an Arab?" thrusting his head out on his stringy neck, inadvertently replicating

Brunhilda's throttled turkey-penis image from scene one.

"What's it to you?"

"You look foreign... and your play here. They're Arab rules. I was playing English chess. Different rules. You see this big one here with the knobbly top?" He picked up his king. "In English rules you can do this..." He leaned across the board and bashed each of his opponent's pieces one by one. Z watched impassively as pieces rolled into his lap and others hit the floor. "There..." Gatlin placed his king at the center of the board. "Checkmate, I believe that's the term." He smirked, arms crossed. But his moment of triumph lasted only as long as it took him to register Z's face. No longer round and avuncular, now square and Neanderthal, those massive jaw muscles set like broken bricks, his head thrust forward to match Gatlin's, his thick neck not so much turkey-penis as Spanish fighting bull.

Gatlin shriveled back in his seat, stunned by his own madness

Why?

He posed the question but had no answer. He'd gone berserk for reason or reasons unknown, and now his wanna-have future, the American-teeth dream, was about to be replaced by the don't-wanna-have nightmare of him crawling back to his hovel with no teeth at all. Then there'd be the aftermath, the reckoning with the Witch, her beefy driver pinning him to a wall while she gutted him with her titanium nails.

And why?

Because he'd thrown a hissy fit.

The bong.

Or rather, the no-bong. It was the only explanation that made sense. That morning smoke had been an integral part of his breakfast-of-champions for years and skipping it had been a dumb move. He'd played it by the book for once. He'd done the right thing. He'd abstained. And this situation—the glowering refrigerator pulsating in front of him—was the direct consequence. That morning toke was essential medication, a THC anchor stabilizing his brain. And today of all days, he'd skipped it. He'd cut the chain and now he was about to crash on the rocks.

Desperate measures were called for...

"Only kidding, mate." He held out his hand for the shake. "I wanted it to look like we were having fun, so no one would ever believe there was anything serious going down."

Z looked at the hand, and Gatlin was expecting one of those big fists to crash into him at any moment. But Z surprised him, uncurling his fists and shaking his hand, a quick shake to be sure, but enough to encourage Gatlin to reach for the newspaper. Z grabbed his wrist just as he touched it, and pain arced up his arm and slammed into his eyeballs. Z didn't so much as squeeze his wrist as roll the bones, crunching and grinding them together as he pulled Gatlin in close.

"I was crowned *baspehlivan*—champion wrestler—at the Kirkpınar, Turkey's annual oil wrestling tournament and the world's oldest sporting event. We don't wrestle oil, *moron*. Combatants cover themselves with olive oil and fight. The object is to grab your opponent and heave him to the ground. Do you have any idea how hard it is to throw a greased-up Turk on his back, especially a fat one wearing only leather undies?"

Gatlin hit information overload: *greased up... leather undies...* that was way too much detail for him. Z loosened his grip and leaned his ear in closer to catch Gatlin's squeaky response, "Only guessing... very hard."

"So you know how easy it would be for me to hurl an ungreased Brit, a puny one with a marshmallow belly and convenient handles on his head, right up on to that roof there." He nodded to a nearby building. It was a ridiculous exaggeration, and in the normal way of things Gatlin would have been stupid enough to call him out on it, maybe even bet him he couldn't and place a wager to back it up. But in view of Z's bone-crunching exhibition, he kept shtum. Suddenly, Z smiled and let him go. It was such an about-face it caught Gatlin on the hop with no idea what to make of it. He rubbed his sore wrist and whimpered.

"What's your real name?" Z said. "Mine's Zaza."

"Gatlin."

"I like you, Gatlin, in a perverse sort of way—"

"I'm not a pervert," Gatlin was quick to note, that image of greased-up Turks rolling around in the dirt a sudden and unwelcome flashback.

"I just mean... it's okay if you're crazy. I spent fifteen years of my life oiling my body up like a shrimp on a barbecue and fighting monstrously savage men. Why? There was no money in it. No global TV audience like football, and oil wrestlers don't get Nike sponsorships either. You'd think the olive oil companies would line up. But they showed me the door. Apparently greasy fat boys slapping each other around is not a *brand enhancer*. So why did I do it? Glory. If that's not crazy, then what is?" Gatlin was relieved to have moved on, but it felt like they'd navigated from a swamp to a quicksand. What explained this sudden gear shift? Why was he being nice to him after grinding his bones? Zaza picked up the newspaper and handed it to him, and Gatlin took it like a wary dog sneaking a scrap of food.

"One last thing... on page two of the newspaper, there is a three-word note, the name of a secure messaging app, a username, and a password. All communication must occur through that channel and only between you and me. This is a nonnegotiable requirement. My principal insists on it. The link goes from her to me and from you to the Ferret. Agreed?"

Gatlin was ecstatic, pain forgotten. Zaza, his new best friend, had just cut the Witch out of the deal.

"That is acceptable," he said, stifling the word *Whoopee!*

"Are you sure you're comfortable with all that stuff? Downloading the app, for example—you're not *rusty* on *downloading*, are you?"

"No, sir. Totally up to speed on the whole loading skill set... uploading, downloading, getting loaded. It's all second nature to me."

Z chuckled artfully. "In that case, go with God, my friend. We'll be in touch."

EIGHT

Gatlin trudged through the overgrown grass at Vistamar, searching for his keys and revisiting his decision to pause his sobriety pledge. Yes, after Zaza's bone-crunching exhibition and with the excitement of seeing all that money, he'd had reasonable cause to partake in a quick snifter. But somehow in the mysterious atmosphere of the Costa Pirate, that had evolved into an overdose event and now he was nursing the consequences. His head was pounding.

Whiskey... hate that stuff.

Gatlin liked to think of himself as a wine connoisseur, and having read somewhere that red wine was good for the heart, he regularly drained a bottle or two for medicinal purposes with his nightly fish and chips. But whiskey!

And that throbbing head wasn't the worst of it.

The master plan?

Where had it gone?

Hatched at a moment of lucidity when his brain had teetered on the pinnacle where madness and genius meet, the master plan had since tumbled into some dark abyss, and however far he reached into the darkness, he found no trace of it. He turned on his phone and it buzzed immediately. He'd turned it off in The Pirate to duck the Witch's calls, but here she was now...

"Well?" she said, her snappy voice reminding him that her instructions had included an immediate confirmation of receipt regarding the money.

"Everything's cool. I've got it."

"Too bad there was no audio... then I could have heard for myself."

"Yeah, he scanned me. No choice about that."

"Okay, good job. I'll come by in an hour or so. We can split up the cash and you can update me."

She hung up.

Odd, that.

Why so nice?

He checked his watch. An hour. Time enough.

With no master plan, there'd be no *go big*. But he still had the fifty thousand, and it wasn't too late to switch plans. That was why he was going home. All he had to do was grab his bag and disappear. He fumbled with his keys in the darkness, then opened the caravan door. It was only a single step up, but Gatlin was so preoccupied with his thoughts, he bungled it, catching his foot and diving headlong through the doorway. Luckily, his head broke the fall, protecting his vital organs by hammering into the cupboard door and sliding down it. For a while, he lay there, wheezing and coughing, neither conscious nor unconscious, floating in his own netherworld.

Then the lights popped on.

He looked up, blinking.

The Witch.

She was standing right next to him, towering over him. She'd been waiting there for him all along.

"Been celebrating, have we?" she said, kicking his legs out of the way so she could slam the door. "Yes, sweetie, we had eyes on you all the way from the beach to the pub, and if you hadn't come back to this dump, you'd now be in a ditch." She made herself comfortable on the sofa. "You want to join me?" She nodded at the bench on the other side of the table.

Gatlin crawled up the cupboard door, pausing halfway to burp up a mouthful of booze, catch it expertly behind his teeth and swallow it back down in a single practiced gulp.

Waste not, want not.

"I brought you a present." She pointed at the gift-wrapped package on the table. "Aren't you going to open it?" She leaned forward, sliding her elbows on the table as he stumbled into the seat opposite and picked up the package. "I think it's just what you need right now."

He ripped open the posh wrapping paper and found a...

Pipe...

And not just any pipe, a work of art fashioned in white, almost translucent, bone china, a woman lying on her back, head up, throat extended, her mouth open, her lips wrapped around a pipe bowl, her feet drawn up towards her buttocks, her knees bent, her legs spread wide enough for a face to fit between them and suck on the discreet mouthpiece concealed as her vagina.

Gatlin's pounding head was momentarily quieted.

"I wanted to get you something to remind you of me... why don't you light it up? You look like you need something to clear your head."

Gatlin was not a man who needed to hear that invitation a second time, especially as he had not yet officially reinstated the pause button. He fetched a bud, ripped it to pieces with his fingers, packed the bowl tight, then paused, his mouth hovering between those porcelain legs.

Was this a pipe of peace?

The symbolism of this luscious idol inviting him to partake of the unholy via the most holy was not lost even on his addled brain. Maybe this was the Witch's way of beckoning him, of extending a welcoming something.

Of course. What else?

Gatlin abandoned his perorations and sucked away, going cross-eyed at one point when his focus snagged on those pure white porcelain nipples and his eyeballs locked up. When he finally took an oxygen break and his normal focus had resumed, the situation had taken a turn for the worst. Gatlin had been issued with a gun by MI6 way back when he'd been their go-to but-haven't-we-got-anyone-else asset. So he knew something about pistols. For example, the difference between a semiautomatic and a revolver, and the gun pointing at him was a revolver.

"Money," she said.

Gatlin put down the pipe and stared at her.

"Money." She cocked the gun.

Gatlin stumbled to his jacket. He pulled the bills out of its secret pocket and put them on the table.

She waved the gun for him to sit and he did so, waiting until she had counted it before going to speak. But she silenced him with a finger to her lips.

No, that wasn't it.

She did tell him to zip it with a *shh*. That was true. But it wasn't why he didn't speak. For some reason, he couldn't. The words wouldn't come out. He wondered about that bud he'd smoked. She'd been here while he was out. She could have spiked it, sprayed it with some fiendish brain-melt shit.

Whoosh...

A lick of flame passed between them.

A magic spell?

Don't be ridiculous.

It was the pot. It had burst into flames.

He looked down at the pipe.

No... it wasn't the pot. It was the pipe itself. Gatlin looked up at her and said, "Grrmghuh," before his eyes went back to the pipe, an exquisite porcelain masterpiece no more, those pointy training-bra titties now dripping off its dwindling torso, those lily-white thighs agape with invitation only moments before now oddly contorted. And so sadly, that inspirational vagina he'd sucked with such vigor was oozing into a—

Wait...!

Gatlin's hands leapt up to his mouth.

"Grmmnnnhuh."

Felicity Drillbit nodded. "That reminds me. I almost forgot to tell you. There was a red alert sticker on the pipe, something about ornamental use only. My Spanish is for shit, but *peligro de incendio* mean anything to you?" Gatlin dashed to the cupboard and ripped open the door. The sacred mirror, the kind one...

"Grrr..."

The mirror had defected, cursed by the Witch, no longer sacred but profane. He stared at the brutal reality of himself and saw a raging old pothead with gummed-up lips. He scraped his nails at the plastic and opened his mouth as wide as he could. But however hard he strained, the lips stayed shut.

Felicity was standing next to him, stroking his withered salt-and-pepper thatch. "C'mon, don't be so down in the mouth." She snickered and pinched his backside. "Look on the bright side. You'll be able to pick it off in a day or two, and in the meantime you can nourish yourself via a nasal drip. Just get one of those blender-thingies, whip up your bacon and eggs into a yummy mush and suck it up your nose with a straw. But now…" She grabbed the back of his neck and dug her nails in deep. "We need to talk." She steered him back towards the table and shoved him into his seat. "Here's your future. Run. You never saw me. You don't know me. None of this ever happened." Gatlin growled and shook his head, pounding the table with his fist. "Not interested?"

He shook his head again, snarling and growling by turns. He would have banged the table again too, but his fist had splatted the molten goddess the first time and was now—from the thermoplastic viewpoint—an integral part of the tabletop.

"Have you spent any of that money I gave you yet?" She waited. But he didn't nod or shake his head. He wondered where this was going. "Did any store you spent it in pass any bills through those little machines they use here?" Oh, oh… now he knew exactly where she was going with this. *That money.* Indeed, he'd spread it far and wide. Lieke's rent demand was just one of the many overdue accounts he'd settled. Thank God he'd used Zaza's money in the pub or Ginger would have called the cops. "You don't think we'd give a creep like you real money, do you?" She waited, but Gatlin didn't even grunt. A miracle had come to pass, and whatever she said now didn't matter a damn. The melted goddess had blessed him with total recall. She had sacrificed herself on a pyre and delivered unto him salvation.

Hallelujah...

The master plan... it was all coming back.

"Don't answer that question," she snickered again. He was going to so love de-snickering her. "Anyway, the bottom line is that the Guardia Civil will be paying you a visit. So it's an ideal moment for you to take a trip." She stood up, taking a single five-hundred-euro note from the stash. "Don't ask me why. Some sort of misplaced maternal instinct, I guess. But I'm going to give you this *real money* to prove that although I'm not really a witch—much as it hurts me to say it—I'm not really the bitch I pretend to be either. I'm just a wonderful actress. So here..." She leaned over him, her breasts swinging in a skintight sweater inches from his face, and tucked it into his pocket. "Breathe deep, little man. Suck those pheromones into your heart... and sigh."

She stood back, her grin vanishing when she saw the photo Gatlin was triumphantly displaying on his phone.

"Mm," Gatlin said, zooming up the photo to show her the Bulgarian plates.

"Give it to me," she said, making a grab for it.

Gatlin stuck the phone under his butt and showed her his fist, the only available one, the other still curled casually on the table where it was pretending not to be stuck.

"I'm not going to pull my gun again. I'm going to negotiate with you, and since that's difficult with your gummed-up lips, I'm going to help you unstick them. All you need to do is open your mouth *really, really* wide"—she curled her hands around the wrist of his glued mitt—"like this"—and yanked it off the table to the sound of ripping flesh and a screaming Gatlin. "Wow… it worked." She sat back and watched as Gatlin conducted a post-trauma toilette, scraping his bloodied lips against his teeth and spitting bits of plastic at her. When he moved on to sucking his wounded hand, she whipped out her gun again. "Okay, so I lied about not pulling my gun."

"And not being a bitch."

"Yeah… that too."

"If I get busted for the counterfeit notes, I'll show the cops that photo."

"What if I pistol-whip you and take the phone?"

"Got a copy online." It wasn't true. But what the heck.

"So you think what… that this is enough to blackmail me into sharing some of this money with you?"

"No, this money's chicken feed. You're going to share the entire kit and caboodle."

She laughed, but not convincingly. "Why would I do that?"

"Because I already cut you out of the deal. All communication is now through an encrypted app. My password. My username. Try and make contact and see how far you get."

"So what if I pistol-whip you into sharing the details?"

"I'll give you the wrong password."

"I'll whip you some more."

"Three times, then the account will implode."

She leapt up, pointing her gun. "You son of a bitch."

"Yeah… that'll work, trying to get it out of me when I'm dead. You need me to set up the final payment." He waited, letting her do the simple arithmetic. "So now we're partners..." He reached for the money.

"Hold on... this has to pay for—"

"What? Who? You and your boyfriend—"

"He's not my boyfriend."

"You two are planning to scam this money. There is no Ferret. You told me yourself. And don't give me that FBI stuff. You're scammers. So now... Felix... you've got a new partner."

She dropped her gun on the seat, slumped next to it and buried her face in her hands. "Megafucked... megafucked."

That was indeed the case, although the extent of her megafuckedness only became apparent some minutes later when her phone rang. She was still moaning to herself at the table while Gatlin was at the sink scrubbing his lips with solvents and scourers.

"I've got an update. Pay attention." Benny Capone's tone did not bode well. She knew from experience that if he was mean and threatening, or even just snarky, all was well with the world. But somber like this, like he was announcing the breakdown in last-ditch peace talks to avert a nuclear war, meant... well, nuclear war.

"I'm listening."

"Père Lachaise... know it?"

"It rings a bell."

"That's where they have to pay the Ferret... the fake Ferret, I mean, That's where the FBI will spring the trap." Felicity was already googling and looking at photos of the biggest cemetery in Paris.

"Where exactly?"

"At the Oscar Wilde tomb."

"They'll be crowds of people there. You expect them to hand over a suitcase full of money at a place like that? They're never going to go for it."

"Maybe it won't be like that. I'll clue you in later."

"So that's all? Wingnut met with the principals already. They want a *when*, a *how*, and a hard number on the money."

"According to the feds, the Ferret's MO is to give details at the last minute so—"

"The money? How can that be last-minute? Like they keep it under their mattress?"

"Jesus, if you try any tricks with this, I'll—"

"You think I'm going to rip you off? I got the FBI waiting around the corner and I got you crawling up my ass with an indictment. So what trick am I supposed to do? Pole vault?"

There was a long pause. Felicity waited it out, listening to his sighs and groans and imagining his bald head shaking in dismay.

"It's not money. It's diamonds."

"The FBI wants diamonds? That's stupid."

"It's something to do with the way they want to prosecute the case. No more than ten cut stones valued at over two million dollars."

Felicity bit her lip. *Two million!*

"And the date?" she said coldly. That drama school might not have worked out in Hollywood, but it was sure paying off now.

"June fifth... but don't ask me how."

"You can tell me. I won't pass it on till the last minute."

"I don't know."

"C'mon, Benny..."

"The FBI won't risk the leak."

"So I go to Paris and—"

"I'll call you. Just keep Wingnut on a leash till then. And make sure you're plenty clear when the shit hits. Things could go wrong. So you need to be out of the firing line. I don't want you calling me from a Paris jail. And by the way, this number's not going to be around to call then anyway. Do this right. I'm giving you a big chance here."

"Thanks, Benny. I owe you." During the conversation, Gatlin had sidled up to her, looking like a photo model on a *Lip Augmentation — What Can Go Wrong* web page.

"I heard the word *money*," he said—at least that was her best guess as, without his lips touching, it was a bit short of consonants.

She didn't want to tell him. But where was that going to go? No Gatlin, no deal.

"Two million," she said sullenly. "In diamonds."

Gatlin sat opposite her. Zaza had said no more than one, but surely that was negotiable.

"Where?"

Felicity packed her gun in her bag. She sat up straight and told him what there was to tell, and what there wasn't. Then she declined his offer of refreshments and left.

Why was she so glum? Gatlin wondered about that. But he soon got over it. The master plan had worked and he had important stuff to do.

Zaza... the message.

Gatlin fired up his phone and opened the secret messenger. He dropped his pants, turned his back to the fickle mirror and bent over, peering at his butt through his legs. The user name he actually remembered, so there was no need to consult his left cheek. But the password was a bitch. Why had Zaza made it so difficult? Numbers and letters were hard enough, but those funny symbols! And the mirror clearly had its own agenda, scrambling them all in the strangest of ways. Was it upside down when he was normal side up, or upside down when he was upside down like now? And how did that affect the back-to-front bit? Gatlin poked in a few numbers before a message reminded him that one more incorrect entry and he'd be locked out for good.

Yipes!

He'd forgotten that. He quit and made himself a cup of tea, and as he drank it, he unpaused the sobriety button, jumping back on the wagon and enjoying a flush of righteousness.

One last shot.

He finished his tea and got a pen and notepad. It was like one of those WWII movies he'd seen as a kid.

Do or die!

For comfort's sake, he stripped naked before bending over with his butt to the mirror and setting to work decrypting the code. He consulted the mirror and, while tuning in to *The Dam Busters* soundtrack playing in his head, he scribbled on the pad on the floor. This was going to be a long and dangerous night.

PART 2

A Poet, a Rock Star, a Zombie and a Cock-Up

NINE

Gatlin was only trying to be helpful. The little boy kicking the back of his seat on the Air Murphy flight to Paris was obviously bored and needed a toy to play with. But when Gatlin gave him a plastic bag with a monster's face drawn on it and told him it was Halloween, all hell broke loose. The brat's mother, a sumo warrior type with a bracelet of swastikas tattooed on both wrists, abandoned her fist-pumping accompaniment to the eye-bulge beat coming from her headset and lobbed a straight right at him.

As Gatlin pointed out to the gendarmes who escorted him off the plane, from that point on, all his actions had been purely self-defensive. In the ensuing kerfuffle—a word that caused a logjam in the interrogation and required the use of a dictionary— she'd inadvertently sat on her boy and gotten her ass wedged between the armrests of his seat. None of this was his fault, he argued, noting that both mother and child were recovering nicely and praising the fire and rescue team that had cut her out. He expressed too sincere regret for having snarled up the airport and the subsequent knock-on delays, which had stretched all the way to New York.

The encounter followed the usual paradigm of Gatlin's interactions with law enforcement. The opening rounds always went to the cops with plenty of *we've nailed you, pal* oozing out of them. But Gatlin was a seasoned arrestee with a doctorate in driving people crazy. And sure enough, their eyes glazed over bit by bit until they were all shuffling around like zombies, mumbling inaudibly and wishing they were the *real* dead instead of the undead. Sooner or later, one of them would have a eureka moment, and they'd pick a junior officer, someone they all hated, to drive him as far as possible out of their jurisdiction.

And so it was this time, all the way to that free ride—the tightwads balked at that and escorted him to the taxi stand instead. Lounging in its back seat, Gatlin turned on his phone. The fight with the sumo Nazi had derailed the plan. *Call me on arrival*, Felix had said before leaving Benidorm days earlier. She'd traveled by car, but even so, she had to be in the city by now.

No need to call... she'd sent a message.

2PM PERE LACHAISE TRAFFIC CIRCLE GAMBETTA CORNER

DON'T BE LATE!!!

He was late, but so was she, picking him up in the Skoda with Dimo at the wheel and driving to a dead-end street neighboring the cemetery, where they parked in the shade of a big plane tree. As the Witch consulted her phone, Dimo got out and sat in the back next to Gatlin. The Bulgarian heavyweight was now carrying a sports bag that Gatlin hadn't noticed before, a big one, big enough for a large gun.

"Nice deserted street...," Gatlin said. "And conveniently located for burying people."

"Don't give me ideas," Felicity said, and then to Dimo, "I got it... off you go."

Dimo's hands disappeared into the bag and emerged not with a gun but with something that looked like a belt with one of those old pagers—an armored edition—welded to it.

"What am I, a dog?" Gatlin said.

Felicity swiveled around and, propping her sunglasses up on her forehead, said, "You want the truthful answer or the polite one?"

Dimo snapped open the GPS tracker and grabbed Gatlin's ankle.

"Come on. We're a team, aren't we?"

"I'd stake my life on it... right up to the point where you get your paws on those diamonds. Think of it as our way of caring. Here..." She checked her phone. "It says so in the manual. *Perfect for that elderly grandpa struggling with dementia*. Plus, with you, there's an added risk. You might get toasted and—"

"I'm on the wagon," Gatlin said.

"Since when?"

"The melting goddess incident... I've got Pot Trauma Stress Disorder. One whiff of the stuff and I get flashbacks."

"So you're still getting tanked?"

"I can't get into the legalese of it."

"The what?"

He shouldn't have mentioned it. There'd be no way to explain the complexities of his sobriety pledge to anyone but a lawyer, although it was clear in his mind. Clause five, subsection C, paragraph (iv) explicitly allowed for herbal tinctures. No beer, no wine, and definitely no whiskey, just an occasional jolt of absinthe, the French decoction whose medicinal value had earned it five-star reviews from aficionados of cool such as Van Gogh.

"Technically... I'm off the sauce."

She looked less than convinced, but she let it go, nodding at Dimo.

"Put it on him," she said before reading the fitting instructions from the manual. Gatlin wriggled a bit. But after Dimo twisted his foot and made him yelp, he calmed down, watching forlornly as the big Bulgarian snapped it on and locked it. Then they ran a test to check it was working with some to-and-fro between them as Felicity checked the monitoring app on her phone.

"We're good," she said, then, turning to Gatlin, "One last thing. Now that we're partners, we need to pool our money. So I'm going to keep it all in our safe where—"

"Forget it. I left it in my room safe already."

"You don't have a room safe. I checked when I booked that room for you." She held out her hand and waited, but all she got from Gatlin was a defiant sneer. "Dimo, I think that bracelet needs tightening a bit." Dimo grabbed Gatlin's leg. "I'll find some really loud music on the radio."

"Okay." Gatlin pulled out a sheaf of bills before either of them could get to work. She eyed it suspiciously and hefted it. "I had the flight and other expenses. What do you expect?" He also had an emergency stash in his underpants. Too bad he hadn't padded that out a bit more.

"You'll get it back, along with your share of the diamonds, after you've picked them up tomorrow."

"So what am I doing at the cemetery today?"

"Just looking around... rehearsals, checking out the poet's grave, getting a feel for the place. Now off you go. And remember"—she tapped her phone—"we're watching you."

With that, they dumped him on the sidewalk, and when the car had disappeared, he fussed with his trouser leg, determined to hide the tracker. But the cloth kept getting caught on it, revealing to all the world that he was an owned man, collared by the Langley Witch. He trudged into the cemetery disconsolate and made his way down an avenue with a long name, something about dead soldiers. Total ignominy. A felon's ankle bracelet on public show. He kept his eyes on the stony road ahead, scanning for dog doo. Dogs were forbidden in the cemetery, but Gatlin was familiar with the ways of the French, and he was taking no chances.

When he arrived at Oscar Wilde's grave, Gatlin stood back from the crowd of visitors, watching them pay their respects by kissing the plate glass that walled off the memorial to protect it from damage. Many of them scribbled love notes on it with lipstick too. Behind the glass was a winged angel on a plinth. Very impressive, Gatlin thought, discovering in his online guide that the statue had originally been hung with massive genitalia, an attribute that Oscar, a noted connoisseur of such, would have no doubt approved. But in the sixties, an envious cemetery bureaucrat had whacked his balls off with a hammer to use as a paperweight. Poor old Oscar, castrated in death as he was figuratively in life. His eyes went down from the angel to his ankle bracelet.

Just like me...

Okay... castration was a stretch. But not much of one. The Witch had sliced the balls off his plan to steal the diamonds. Sooner or later, he'd have to cut that damn bracelet off, and that meant finding a tool. Gatlin was scheduled to pick up the diamonds the following day, then meet with the Witch. So what he needed was a jailbreak between those two events when he'd lose the tracker, an ejector-seat-button moment, where he could bail out like DB Cooper, never to be seen again. He left Oscar to his fans and walked around aimlessly.

How absurd was it? He was just one ankle bracelet away from his dream. If he could just find a way to—

The screech of a chainsaw teleported him back to that fateful night in Brunhilda's villa, a horrifying moment, but it was short-lived, replaced by a revelation.

Chainsaw!

There it was... a beefy man was wielding it and hacking into an overgrowth of shrubs.

That chainsaw would make short work of...

Gatlin considered the operation, looking back and forth between the saw, chomping through branches of approximately ankle-bone thickness, and the skintight bracelet on his ankle. Theoretically, there were two options. *Saw the foot off* had a lot going for it in terms of speed and simplicity, but the downside—crawling out of the cemetery on his hands and knees and leaving a trail of blood—made it a no-no. As for option two—cutting off the bracelet—Gatlin had to admit that, given his surgical skills, that approach was most likely to end up with the same outcome as option one.

Too bad. Wrong tool. But right idea. And the right place too. The cemetery was huge and needed plenty of maintenance. There had to be some sort of tool here somewhere that would work without crippling him. He walked on until he reached the crematorium, where he stopped. It was a strange-looking building, the ugly offspring of a church and a power plant with arches, pillars, a dome and two chimneys tapering up to heaven. Gatlin was wandering around at the back of the building, hoping to stumble on a worker with a suitable tool, when voices stopped him. They seemed to come from nowhere until two men appeared in front of him, rising up out of the ground. Gatlin hurried forward as they headed off the other way, finding steps leading down to a basement.

He trotted down them, caught the door as it was closing and slipped inside into an empty corridor. There were doors on both sides, and he went from door to door, listening at each before trying the handle. They were all locked, until halfway down when a handle turned and he cracked the door wide enough to verify that the room was empty. He entered and shut the door behind him.

Coffins... no surprise there, caskets on tables with their lids off.

There were only two cupboards, but sadly, no tools in either, just bottles of chemicals with names long enough to fill the entire label. Gatlin peeked inside one of the coffins, heaving with relief to discover it was empty. He checked the rest, driven by morbid interest.

They were all empty, an assembly line of coffins waiting for nature to take its course and provide suitable content. Some were plain, others ornate, the dead segregated into rich and poor as in life. Each coffin had a label with a sales pitch in eight languages. Gatlin read a few, wondering what kind of box he'd end up in.

One model, called Green Comfort, was not only cheap but environmentally friendly as it was made of biodegradable cardboard. He was all but sold on that one until he realized that it meant the worms would get to him that much sooner. The bestseller, according to the label, was a budget option in a flat-pack, which had the added benefit of reducing your carbon footprint, a noted concern of the dead.

Gatlin checked the corridor before trying the remaining doors, but they were all locked. So he moved on, exiting the building and giving up on the cemetery. It was huge, and he didn't have the time. Besides, he'd had an idea: a hardware store or DIY center, a *quincaillerie*, according to his translate app.

He soon found one in the 20th and plotted a route on his phone map. But it was hard to follow. The sun had come out, making it impossible to read the screen. He stepped into the doorway of a pâtisserie to get some shade, and as he was fingering and zooming, a passing motor scooter caught his attention, howling like a food mixer and belching putrid smoke. He peeked out into the street as it skidded to a halt.

Two young men. Scruffy. Up to no good from the look of them.

Gatlin edged back into the doorway, where he could check them out unseen. The passenger hopped off the moped and it sped off. The man took an each-way glance before reaching under his jacket and pulling out a bolt cutter, a fancy one with telescopic handles, which he opened up full-length before disappearing behind a parked van. Gatlin cursed himself as he tiptoed towards the thief. Why hadn't he thought of that? Europe was the global epicenter of bike theft, with millions of stolen two-wheelers ending up on the streets of the Ukraine and all points east. He should have just waited by a rack with a—

"Nice bike," he said, looking down at the crouching man wrestling with its chain. The bike looked like a prop in a sci-fi movie and it was locked with a heavy chain covered in a cut-resistant fabric to a rack. "Jam one handle against the curb, then use your foot on the other." Gatlin mimed his advice for added clarity.

The man jumped up, pointing the bolt cutter threateningly. But he soon got the message when Gatlin waved cash at him and pointed to the bolt cutter. The thief looked from Gatlin's ankle bracelet to the bills in his hand. Quite a pile. Many times what the bolt cutter was worth. Then he glanced at the bike with its stubborn high-tech chain cover. Without a word, he took the money and handed over the bolt cutter.

Gatlin didn't hesitate. He crouched, yelping like a Chihuahua when his knees crunched into bent mode. Then he slid the chain between the blades, jammed one handle into the crook of the curb and leaned on the other with his full weight. The blades snapped through the chain and he pitched onto the sidewalk.

The thief made a move to get the bike but Gatlin jumped up. He had the bolt cutter now and he waved it aggressively. It was his bike. He'd stolen it. He was, however, prepared to negotiate. He rubbed his thumb and index finger together. The thief tilted his head back and puckered his lips. And for one horrible moment, Gatlin thought he might kiss him. But then he turned it into that haughty, down-the-nose look that makes the French feel better when they're getting shafted. He handed over the money.

Gatlin gave him the bike and headed back to the cemetery with the bolt cutter hidden under his coat. There wasn't much time. It was closing time soon, and he had to hide his prize. Luckily, he'd spied a spot earlier that was suitable, if only he could...

Yes, he found it, a grassy area with white lines laid out in neat rows. They reminded him of chalk boundary lines in cricket. But what kind of sport did they play in a cemetery? The lines were so close too, only a couple of feet apart. Running lines? he speculated, although for very small people. He found a quiet area behind a lone tree that was perfect. He kicked away the chalky paint lines, took out his bolt cutter and hacked a hole in the turf. Kneeling next to it, he dropped the bolt cutter into it and packed clumps of grass on top of it. Pleased with his work, he stepped out from behind the tree only to see a uniformed man with a stick standing on the pathway. The man waved his stick and shouted.

Gatlin looked over both shoulders.

Moi?

The man answered his unvoiced question with a booming...

"Interdit."

Forbidden... the word was well-known to Gatlin as it was the preferred term of most French when they encountered him. As for this man's hysterics, seriously... for walking on the grass.

"C'est une terre consacrée. Les cendres des morts sont là."

Gatlin nodded agreeably, though uncomprehendingly, the word *morts* being familiar. Wasn't that written on a lot of those tombstones?

The man's face switched from anger to stupefaction as Gatlin got closer, his mouth opening wide as if Gatlin was lobbing him nuts and he was determined to catch one. He dropped his cane and Gatlin followed his glazed eyeballs all the way to his own black Nikes. Only they weren't black anymore. They were white, like his pants where he'd been kneeling.

Ash!

So that was the story. The rich got fancy coffins and memorials, the upwardly mobile got bio-boxes, and the *does-your-deceased-have-a-coupon* crew got spray-painted on the grass by a muck spreader. Gatlin had messed up. If he'd pissed on the French flag, it could hardly have been worse, and now the angry Frenchman was working the phone, calling a posse.

Maybe they'll find the bolt cutter!

This was yet another crisis calling for desperate measures. If only he were the British prime minister, he could call an emergency meeting with his top ministers, so they could talk about *how to fix it* for as long as possible, or at least as long as it took the Americans to actually fix it.

Panic came to his rescue with a lightning bolt of inspiration. He slapped his hand on his left breast, and broke into song:

"Allons enfants de la Patrie

Le jour de gloire est arrivé!"

Yes, Gatlin's schoolboy French did not cover essentials like how to ask for directions to the toilet, but worthless crap like the French national anthem had been drilled into his DNA. The man responded as if under remote control, abandoning his phone call and standing to attention. He even joined in on the chorus, although he did get one of the lines wrong, a faux pas for which Gatlin excused him in the spirit of the Entente Cordiale.

The man held out both arms as they finished in sync.

A hug, Gatlin thought, but...

Jesus, no.

The man kissed him. Both cheeks. Big wet garlicky whoppers.

Gatlin took it like a man, albeit a French one.

Diamonds... think of the diamonds.

TEN

It was all happening in the 20th, the Paris district known not only for its famous cemetery but for its mix of bustling streets and gentrified villages. The Ferret was already ensconced in its lair on one of those streets, an artisan's workshop with a courtyard, hidden by garage doors covered with tattered posters and peeling paint.

As Gatlin was hurrying back to his hotel from the cemetery, the Ferret was opening a special package from China, a rush delivery from Wuhan. She—it was the second of the month—had spent time there posing as a buyer for a pest control company, and her trail had led her to the manufacturers of XRAT, a new poison developed to combat the so-called maxrats that plagued the Chinese province. The outcome of a genetic experiment gone wrong, they were a cross between a brown rat and a Tibetan mastiff. The resulting animal averaged sixty pounds in weight and had canines that grew forever on either side of guillotine-like incisors.

When a pair of these impressive beasts had escaped, not a word was leaked to the media, with the authorities adopting a wait-and-see attitude.

They didn't have to wait long. The maxrats soon proved that big teeth were not the only characteristic they shared with their rodent ancestors. They bred like them too, and since they were meat eaters, they had already solved Wuhan's stray dog problem. This, and the dwindling number of homeless littering the streets, was seen as a benefit by the Chinese Communist Party and fully aligned with their strategy on social reform. So still nothing had been said. There'd been rumors, of course, and that spike in the number of children missing on their way home from school should have been picked up by someone. But it was only when an entire rural classroom disappeared, pupils and teachers both, that it hit the fan. Some of the parents were big shots in the Party, so heads had to roll and a solution be found. XRAT was the answer, a poison adapted from a biological weapon. The Ferret took a single vial of this doom-juice out of the package.

Is it enough?

She glanced up at her planning wall, where a life-sized photo of president Rump hung next to one of a maxrat. Dosage was critical. What did POTUS weigh? About two-forty-plus. But what if he'd been bingeing his Big Macs? The Ferret went to her computer and made the calculation.

Rump equals... the actual number was five point five, but she decided to up the dose. Best not to cut corners. The Ferret moved on to her delivery system. This, unlike the poison, was not new. The Ferret had designed it years earlier, but it had been too brilliant to waste on a run-of-the-mill victim. It called for a special occasion like this, the Cadillac of kills.

She fiddled with the mechanics and electronics. It was complex, with so much to go wrong. Mechanically, it was an air pistol firing a dart. The problem was the dart. It was a splinter of ice. Or more exactly, a frozen sliver of XRAT. To keep the dart from melting, the loading chamber of the gun had to be surrounded by dry ice. All this complexity came at a price. There was a lot of stuff in this weapon, way too much for a gun.

Besides, that would be found by security or spotted before it could be used. But the Ferret had a plan for all that. The dart would hit the president and he'd wince. There'd be a small puncture wound like a wasp sting, but little blood. He'd brush it off maybe, make some macho gesture, anxious to show that some French bug had no chance of making him cry. He'd continue with the ceremony. Then *bam*... he'd have a stroke and hit the deck like one of the fine old buildings he used to implode to build one of his ugly hotels. She surveyed the wall, three photos in total, consulted her chart and scribbled their fatal doses in red across their hearts...

SEWER RAT (*Rattus norvegicus*) x 0.02 units
MAXRAT (*Rattus maximus*) x 1.00 units
RUMP (*Rattus praesidis*) x 6.66 units
The Ferret licked her lips.

On the other side of Paris, Zaza was licking his lips too. It was inadvertent and he would have reprimanded himself for doing so had he noticed, but he was far too engrossed in the object of his attention for that.

He was in the kitchen of Eve's residence, a Directoire mansion in the 16th district, the Trocadéro, the posh part of town. He'd often dropped her off and picked her up there, but on those occasions he'd only gotten as far as the courtyard. Now he'd had the tour, ending up in the kitchen where Eve was cooking him an omelet. Lots of good things in it too. Although it wasn't the aroma of her prawn pad Thai mix that had him licking his lips. It was rather the sight of her ass as she reached over the island for a knife to matchstick the carrots, her tiny body arching and stretching, calves bunching, thighs tightening, her heels lifting to tiptoe.

"A new experience for you, I think," she said. He sucked his tongue back into his face just in time as she swiveled towards him and winked. "The prawn pad Thai omelet, I mean... it's one of my specialties."

"Looking forward to it," he said, sounding oddly perky.

Prawn pad? He had no idea.

Surely it wouldn't be in the same league as...

Meatballs.

He licked his lips some more as he watched her chop vegetables with machinelike precision.

"How'd it go?" she said.

"I planted every last one." Zaza had spent hours in the cemetery placing cameras at strategic locations, secreting them in bushes or sticking them under recycling bins with magnets.

His phone rang. He checked it and was about to drop it back in his pocket when Eve said, "Is it her? You can take it in the office if you need privacy. This'll be a few minutes yet."

He didn't want privacy. He wanted to drop the phone back in his pocket and drop his wife any which way there was. But Eve had this rom-com fantasy idea about them. How brutal he'd be to burst that bubble. And besides, Beverly was his excuse, his protector. He couldn't stop thinking about Eve, and not in ways his Koran-thumping wife would be sympathetic towards.

He hurried down the hallway, bundling his dreams and his nightmares and booting them out of sight. He knew where the office was, having had the tour, but he stopped in an alcove next to a tall neoclassical vase set on a table. This was far enough, out of sight and out of earshot at least. He went to make the call, but the phone rang again before he had the chance.

"I'm so excited," Beverly said, the words bursting out of her, her voice bubbly, reminding him of the old Beverly, the fun one with the killer right hook. "I got the word today. I just need a teensy-weensy bit of help at the border—"

"In Turkey?"

"And a wee bit of cash."

"They said yes?"

"There's only one condition. I know you're going to say no, but they insist that—"

"Money? They want money?" That was way too enthusiastic, like he was already pulling out his wallet. He gave himself a virtual rap on the knuckles.

"Divorce... they say I have to divorce you. They will only accept me if I'm free to marry a warrior and bear his children."

That sounded like good news, but it was a downer. Even a quickie divorce would take months of paperwork. He'd been hoping she could get a plane later that day.

"Please forgive me for breaking your heart," she said.

Zaza's big moment... *act heartbroken*.

He sniffed and whimpered. But before he could utter his stuttering response, she said, "I know it's going to be a terrible shock for you. But I've been discussing this with the imam"—that had to be the fire-and-brimstone one—"and he's agreed to backdate the paperwork. It'll be a Sharia divorce. But that's all we need. These guys don't give a damn about French law.

But you need to call him to okay everything. So I'm begging you, my darling…"

Zaza lowered the phone and covered it as Eve appeared in the hallway. She said nothing. Just a wink, a smile, and a beckoning finger. Dinner was ready. She wiped her hands on her apron, down by her thighs, and he watched as she spun around and headed back to the kitchen, his eyes following the sway of her butt.

That was what did it, the swish and sway of it all. Zaza's gears shifted, and he put the phone back to his mouth, his Academy Award performance done with.

"What's the imam's number?" He noted it down. "Got it. Book the next flight to Turkey. Anywhere will do. I'll have you met at the airport and safely smuggled across the border to meet with your new friends."

Zaza wasted no time following up on that. And coincidentally, as the phone rang in the radical imam's mosque, the alarm rang on the Ferret's phone. She was still plotting and planning in her lair, and she'd set it earlier. She wanted to get to the cemetery before it closed, so she could check the relevant tombs like a steeplechase jockey walking a track to eyeball the jumps the day before the race. This was essential. Tomorrow she'd get the diamonds and that had to go right.

No diamonds, no kill, no glory.

She hurried out, scurrying through backstreets to the cemetery where she picked her way through graves to the tomb of Victor Noir, her mind fast-forwarding to the moment she'd get those diamonds.

She'd always been paid in cash or crypto before, but this time was different. This was to be her final kill, her crowning achievement, and those diamonds were destined for a crown. She'd have it made by a jewelry artisan, a gold crown set with diamonds so she could wear the death of the president on her head. Not in public, of course. But privately, alone at home while she was watching her favorite soaps.

She looked down at the bronze effigy of Victor Noir, the cemetery's only murder victim, reliving his tempestuous years in the shadow of the French Revolution in her mind. Born a Jew, Victor had converted first to Catholicism and then to flat-out crazy. Ironically, it had all started with fake news. At least, Pierre Bonaparte said it was fake. So he challenged the alleged fake-news journalist to a duel. The wily hack accepted and sent his buddy, crazy Victor, to fix the time and place. But that didn't happen because Victor got in a punch-up with Little Boney, who shot him dead.

Reportedly, Victor had a revolver in his pocket but never got to use it, and the sculptor who cast his bronze effigy certainly believed that story. He'd made a literal point of it, styling an impressive bulge in Victor's pants pocket. But that gun-in-the-pocket theory had been rejected by Parisian women in favor of a more biological interpretation. And in the years since, seeking the blessing of fertility, they had stroked Victor's pocket pistol with such fervor they'd rubbed off the green suit of corrosion that shrouded the rest of his body, creating a phallic bump that glinted golden in the late sun.

"Victor," the Ferret murmured before looking over both shoulders. There was no one around. She'd gotten lucky. Victor was one of the cemetery's star attractions with his own channel on YouTube. She'd even caught a few videos herself. She shivered with disgust as she recalled them... poor Victor, the way those women had defiled him.

Although...

She wrestled a should-I-shouldn't-I moment before curiosity got the better of her and she stepped up onto the pedestal.

Another look over both shoulders...

Nobody.

The Ferret climbed up and sat astride his hips.

Tricky, this.

The Ferret had never known man or woman in the biblical sense, so she was flying blind, shifting her butt around in an exploratory fashion. Yes, this was a major downside to being an it—*where the fuck is the G-spot?*

"Oh, Victor...," she said, faking a few moans, a technique she'd picked up watching *Sex and the City*. "Help me, and I'll send you a friend: President John Thomas Rump. Bestow your blessings on me... your fecundity." She stopped. That word had sounded so good, so naughty. She said it again as she slumped forward, their faces now inches apart.

Wait a minute...

Victor's whole face was shiny, not just his lips, the green stripped off his entire face. That wasn't right. That wasn't correct protocol. You were supposed to stroke his penis, or sit on it if you must, and kiss his lips. Not fuck his face. Those dirty YouTube bitches had been sitting their fat asses on it. She went to kiss him anyway, but pulled up sharp. First and foremost, there was the hygiene issue. From their asses to her face was not a comforting picture. But beyond that, maybe those girl-girls knew what they were doing. They knew where their G-spots were. Maybe his face was the right place.

She paused, glancing around one last time.
Still no one.
In for a penny...
She crawled up his body and went to work.

As the Ferret was enjoying her man, Felicity Drillbit was getting ready to kill hers, although she didn't yet know it. She was lying on the bed in her panties and bra, touching up her nails and waiting for Benny's call when she remembered the recording she'd made during the afternoon pump-and-grind session with Dimo. She was not in the habit of recording such events, especially not one as dull as this. But desperate for entertainment—and just for fun—she'd opened the translate app on her phone and turned on the mike to catch some of his dirty talk. She took her phone off the nightstand and fitted her earbuds.

Dimo was busy in the bathroom taking selfies of his six-pack—but he'd left the door open, and she wanted to enjoy this recap privately. Who knew what the translate app would make of it?

The recording played automatically, and there it was: the twang of cheap springs under their pulsating bodies, her own encouraging—and expertly faked—groans, and Dimo's passionate, gritty...

"One-two-three-four—"

She got up slowly, her studied calm terrifyingly real, and walked to the safe.

"Thirty-three, thirty-four..."

She opened the safe and reached inside, her hand coasting over the pile of money and seizing the rubber grip of her Colt Cobra.

"Fifty-seven, fifty-eight..."

She hefted it. *Nice.* Dimo might have the muscles, but she had the difference.

But now what?

Bursting into the bathroom and blasting holes in his six-pack was tempting. But in the end—"Hundred and six, hundred and seven..."—she decided to wait, gun held loosely behind her back, and sometime after his breathless "two hundred seventy-seven, two hundred and seventy-eight... aargh...," he emerged from the bathroom.

"Two hundred seventy-eight?" she said.

He grinned. "Isn't it wonderful? I never even get to two hundred with anyone else."

She showed him the gun with the barrel only an inch from his eyeball, so he'd be sure to notice. He stopped grinning and started twitching.

"Let me explain something, Musclenuts. It's miserable enough getting fucked like a rowing machine. But to actually be regarded as a rowing machine by a lover brings out my... feminazi reflexes." She cocked the Cobra. *"Au revoir, mon amour."*

Dimo fell to his knees, hands together, transformed into a pleading supplicant.

"You are goddess. You are special. It's truth. I swear. My wife is only sixty-two."

"Your wife?"

He nodded. "Due to medical condition." His face fell as he caught his faux pas. He'd told her he was single. "Not exactly wife. I call her wife. But really is sister."

Felicity lowered her gun. This was getting too crazy even for her. And while she was searching for a suitable retort, the phone called time on their confrontation.

She pointed to the bathroom with her gun.

"Get in there and don't come out till I tell you to, or I'll shoot you."

She tossed the gun on the bed and grabbed her phone as he disappeared.

"Benny, sweetie..."

"The president flies out of Washington on the fifth and—"

Felicity let him ramble on. This was the last time she'd ever speak to him, a moment to savor. Yes—the Witch of Switch was about to transform herself yet again. After tomorrow, there'd be no more Benny, no more Dimo. As soon as she had those diamonds, she'd—

"Finally, there's one important point." Benny paused after saying it and that pulled her up sharp, a long tick-tock pause that told her a bomb was about to go off. "There won't be a person-to-person payoff at the tomb. It has to be a drop."

A drop!

"What the hell are you saying?"

"They'll be no human-to-human contact."

"That's okay. I'm sending Wingnut."

"No, including him."

"So how do we do it?"

"They'll be a drop box or something. They're going to contact me tomorrow morning your time, so it'll be in the middle of the night here."

"You said it would be easy. I send Wingnut to pick up a bag—"

"I know... *and he gets arrested*, I said that. But what's it to you anyway? Why are you so uptight about this?"

"Nothing." She dialed it back, stifling a scream.

"I'll call you tomorrow morning with exact instructions."

When Felicity set the phone aside, she slumped on the bed, her anger simmering.

No one-to-one. What, then?

Dimo's wailing plea interrupted her thoughts. "Is okay? Please, don't shoot."

"Stay there, you bastard."

She'd need him a little longer, but she'd let him sweat out the night.

Tomorrow?

It was coming down to a prayer and a hope.

She stuck the Cobra in her panties, curled up in a ball and reached for the light.

ELEVEN

On June 5, 2019, when the Père Lachaise cemetery opened at nine, the first group through the Gambetta entrance included an old man, an invisible man, camouflaged by age and appearance, a man who seemed as much a part of the setting as the tombstones, a man visiting a deceased wife perhaps, a fallen friend, or a child who had passed before his time.

The man walked with a limp, dragging one leg like it was a dead weight. He had no map, unlike the tourists who scattered this way and that, hurrying to cross another item off their must-do-in-Paris list. As the crowd cleared, the man turned left and paused at the Memorial Gardens, catching his breath as he admired the flowers. He turned down Avenue Carette and walked as far as the resting place of Oscar Wilde, where he sidled up to a neighboring grave whose tombstone, a slab of granite in the shape of a coffin, served as a sofa for the Irish writer's visitors.

The two memorials were so close the young woman currently seated there could reach Oscar's glass barrier. The old man waited while she wrote her message and left. Then he took her place as though suddenly tired and in need of rest. He held his left hand on his chest and rocked forward, placing his right hand on the glass barrier for support.

That was all.

No scribbling, no hearts, no numbers.

But as he stood up, he glanced down at the glass where the stencil on his palm had been transferred by the heat of his hand. It was next to the girl's lipstick scribble. She'd written a quote from the poet: *Every saint has a past, and every sinner a future*. The Ferret chuckled, a sniffle of sound and a ripple of movement under all the old-man prosthetics. Saint or sinner, someone with no future was the US president. The message he'd left, a simple heart in Day-Glo pink with an inscription inside, was nothing other than the epitaph of President John Thomas Rump.

His work here done, the Ferret headed towards the Reunion exit and stopped when he reached a quiet section.

No one famous buried here. No one around.

He double-checked, then disappeared behind a giant tombstone hidden by a canopy of branches and leaves. He took out a burner phone, attached a file containing the payment instructions to a terse message and hit the send button. An hour or two later he'd get the reply, the green light, and it would be time to visit Victor Noir's tomb and pick up the jewels that would adorn his crown.

In New York, Benny's phone chirped the Ferret's message.

It's the middle of the night, dammit.

Not exactly, but any time before dawn was the same thing to Benny. He was not a sunrise guy. Unless it was the tequila variety in the company of a pneumatic blond. Those he could handle, but the tail end of a bleak Manhattan night with most of it spent searching unsuccessfully for a loophole in New York's fifty-fifty divorce law made for an especially grouchy wake-up call.

NOW

His hands trembled. It was really happening. He sat up on the bed and opened the file. The instructions were crazy complicated. So he read them twice, shaking his head. The Witch would go apeshit when he told her, but too bad. The Ferret was calling the shots. He slipped on a silk dressing gown and took the phone into the living room, where he stood by the window, looking down at Central Park and the lights of Manhattan. His other phone—his official phone—was on the coffee table. Its screen lit up with an incoming call, but he ignored it.

His wife.

She always called several times during the night—every time she took a piss most likely—a guerrilla warfare tactic, hoping he'd forgotten to mute his phone so she'd wake him up. He turned it off completely.

The Witch call was too important to risk distractions. She was the weak link. He had to shore that up. She had to believe the FBI story, so she'd stay the fuck away. The Ferret had to get those diamonds. Way back when they'd actually been planning a fake assassination, Felicity had been a perfect choice—a born actor with a rap sheet as long as one of her plastic schlongs and a pending indictment to incentivize her cooperation. But now? She'd have only one thing on her mind: how to grab those diamonds and escape the FBI. He went back to his view at the window—it made him feel big to see all the tiny cars and people—and placed the call.

Felicity listened to Benny's sales pitch, maintaining a fake, ice calm, girding herself for what was to come.

"This is out of my hands," he said. She could all but see his theatrical gesture, throwing his arms up in the air perhaps, or shrugging his shoulders. "The feds are calling the shots."

He hadn't told her jack yet and already he was on the defensive.

"So how's it go?"

"The Ferret has... I mean the FBI, the fake Ferret has drawn a heart on the barrier of that writer's grave. Oscar... the famous fag. You check it out like I told you?"

"Already did."

"So you know it's a hotspot hangout for weirdos?"

Felicity remembered the lipstick graffiti on the barrier, but this still wasn't making sense.

"So what's with the heart? They all draw hearts."

"Yeah, I know it's a thing. That's the point. It's like a leaf hidden in a tree. It disappears. But the fake-Ferret heart is different. It has writing in it."

"So do all the rest of them. Love notes. Arrows."

"But not numbers."

"Like a code... a safety deposit?" That got her excited. Lots of possibilities there.

"Two numbers with a slash between them. The first is the cemetery section, and the second is the grave number inside the section. They've got to leave a bunch of white lilies with the diamonds. Kinky, eh? Real old-school Cold War stuff."

"Why so complicated?"

"Maybe it fits the Ferret's MO and the feds know it. Who cares? All you got to do is message Coronata. She's got to check out Oscar's tomb, then drop the lilies at whatever other grave it points to—"

"And when Wingnut shows up to make the pickup, the cops jump on him?"

"Something like that..."

Something fishy, more like. The real Ferret was the Scarlet Pimpernel of assassins, famed for deception and subtlety. Felicity could see him hatching a plan like this. But why would the FBI bother? That didn't sound right. But she couldn't see what was wrong with it. In any case, what did it matter? These were the cards on the table and she had to play the hand. "So as soon as you get the message through to Coronata, let me know."

"Why? The FBI will be waiting there anyway, won't they?"

"Sure they will. But I want to know how it's going. I need to inform the president. So keep me in the loop, eh? Be a buddy."

Felicity's eyes zoomed wide...

Buddies?

There was something fishy about that too, but her mind skipped on past it in the clear light of an opportunity.

Numbers in a heart pointing to a grave...

So what if she replaced the numbers? What if they pointed to *her* grave, a tomb far from the FBI trap? The diamonds would be hers, and she could eliminate the Wingnut risk by picking them up herself. She finished up the call with her eyes on Dimo. He was lying on a rubber mat doing stomach crunches. He'd been so crawly and sycophantic after she'd let him out of the bathroom, she'd almost forgiven him for real. But now he could earn his keep and run an important errand.

"It's on," she said.

He leapt up and wriggled into a T-shirt two sizes too small.

"I'm ready," he said, checking himself out in the mirror and puffing up his chest. "Born ready."

She wanted to slap him every time he said that. But she sucked it up and pressed ahead, shapeshifting from feminazi into maiden in distress.

"Everything depends on you, my darling. Thank God you're such a manly man."

"Understood."

"You have to go to the writer's tomb, the one we checked out."

"The angel with no balls?"

"Exactly." She'd belabored that point when they'd checked out the tomb, confident a castrated angel would be a memorable enough image to avoid any mistakes. She went on to describe a heart with two numbers divided by a slash as Benny had explained, but she could see Dimo's eyes glazing over and knew she couldn't risk this on his limited intelligence. It had to be idiotproof, and her many years of servicing males had convinced her that when it came to idiocy, men were extremely resourceful. So she made it simpler. "Take a photo."

"Of the heart—"

"And send it to me. Then, erase the heart." His brow furrowed. "Rub it out." She made a fist and jiggled it back and forth. "You understand?"

"What with?"

That was how hard this work was—*what with!*

"It's lipstick, you dummy. Why don't you lick it off to see how it tastes?" She groaned, turning it into a laugh when she saw his eyes narrow with mistrust. She still needed him. She took a breath and waited a beat for the moment to pass. "So after you rub off the heart, you draw a new one. Hold on…"

She snapped open a laptop and pulled up a visitor's map of the cemetery that listed all the celebrities buried there with their graves marked and numbered. She read through the names of the dead. None were familiar, although some rang a faint bell. Each of the deceased was listed together with his or her occupation. "I thought they were celebrities… important people. Most of these are just writers." She wanted a name she knew and soon found one: Jim Morrison, singer with the Doors. But she soon rejected the sixties rocker. The tomb would be crawling with lowlife Americans, sleazebags who'd steal a good-looking bunch of flowers even if they didn't know about the diamonds. "Edith Piaf." She checked the map. "Perfect."

"Who's she?"

"Another junkie singer. They made a movie about her. The Little Sparrow, they called her. In France, she's a saint. Up there with Joan of Arc."

The cool thing about Piaf's grave was the location, section ninety-seven, right in the corner between two entrances and close to the wall.

97/52

She sent him the message so he had it on his phone.

"Got it?"

"Ninety-seven, fifty-two."

"Written like that. In a heart. Then you take a photo of this new heart and you send it to me."

"So I send you two photos?"

She so wanted to slap him. Instead, she explained it one more time before dispatching him on his mission.

She watched from the window as he made his way down the street, then checked her watch, her mind moving on.

Gatlin?

She checked his location on her GPS bracelet app.

He was still at the hotel. She had to call him soon, but with her plans still fuzzy, that could wait. The priority now was replacing the Ferret/FBI heart with her Edith Piaf heart and setting up the switcheroo.

Only streets away in a poky pension, Gatlin had woken early and breakfasted on a leftover snack from the day before, stale croissant and cold coffee.

Suitably nourished, he opened the window and puffed his chest in and out a few times in what he believed to be a yoga breathing exercise, albeit interrupted by a ball of something slimy that appeared in his mouth and had to be spat out in the bathroom and scrutinized lest it contained any sign of a living creature.

Vivified by Parisian prana and oblivious to its stench of drainage and moped-exhaust fumes, Gatlin was a new man. This was the day and he wasn't going to foul it up. He closed the window and went to the bathroom, where he stood in front of the mirror to deliver a pep talk.

The bathroom was minuscule, and so was the hotel room beyond it, but it was only a few blocks from Père Lachaise, so he had time to get organized and get pumped. At the end of this day, he'd be richer than he'd ever imagined with enough ready money to live the life of a king.

Totally pumped, he checked his phone. No news. At some point, he'd be getting a call. Two, in fact. One from the Witch, and one from Zaza. Until then, he had time to kill. *Not good. Dangerous, even.* Weaknesses were Gatlin's forte. So when the devil went looking for idle hands, Gatlin was always the first in line. And this was the bewitching hour, that moment after breakfast when the body was fortified and the mind hopeful, but the spirit weak. No way could he wobble—not today. So to keep the devil at bay, Gatlin sat on the bed and checked the map of Père Lachaise on his phone, skimming through its list of celebrity tombs until he got to... Jim Morrison, the rock star who reinvented himself as a poet in Paris.

I'd been down so bloody long
That it looked like up to me

Gatlin sang a few lines. He'd visited the grave in the seventies. Back then, it had been a simple affair where a few freaks would hang out smoking dope, never forgetting to leave a spliff for the rock poet.

A spliff for Jim...

Gatlin googled a bit, learning how the grave had gotten a headstone in the eighties and how its bust had been stolen and the whole place trashed and defaced with graffiti. In the end, they'd replaced everything and put up barriers.

A spliff for Jim?

Gatlin couldn't get that out of his head. Were young freaks as kind and generous as the freaks of yore? But what about that *idle hands* stuff and his sobriety pledge? He was so into that he'd left Benidorm without so much as a tiny bud. Gatlin struggled with a convincing sales pitch on the one hand and on the other, a get-thee-behind-me doggedness that shocked him, especially when it almost won the debate. In the end, there was a negotiated settlement. He would *not* go down to Jim Morrison's tomb hoping to scrounge a spliff, but he would go there to pay his respects and kill some time. The Witch had told him to stay put in the hotel, but surely the cemetery wasn't off-limits. He had to go there later anyway, and he could say he was doing extra research while waiting for her call.

Minutes later, he was out the door.

TWELVE

Felicity's phone rang.

"I've found the heart," Dimo said.

"You remember what to do?"

"I am not an idiot."

Felicity dodged the issue, plowing away with her recap and emphasizing the need to take the photo of the heart before erasing it rather than after. When the call was done, she waited for the photo.

92/50

That was the grave number written in the FBI/Ferret heart. She went to her laptop and was soon thumbing through Wikipedia's account of the life of Victor Noir. *What an asshole!* To get shot arranging a duel where someone else was supposed to get shot required a talent for blundering that was exceptional even among males. Inevitably, that line of thinking led her to Gatlin, although there was little point in calling him until she'd heard from Dimo and he'd confirmed that the switcheroo Edith Piaf grave heart had replaced the FBI/Ferret's Victor Noir tomb. So she waited, shuffling through Google images of the relevant tombs, and following up on Victor's shiny dick... pages and pages of images...

Only the French.

Gatlin entered Père Lachaise by the same gate as the day before, and when he checked his map, he discovered that Jim Morrison's grave was at the other end of the cemetery. Not to worry. It was a fine day with the sun threatening to bust through the gray clouds at any moment, and he was enjoying the promenade. After reviewing several routes, he took the Circular Avenue. It was longer, but easier. So at least he wouldn't get lost. He strutted off. He didn't have the diamonds yet, but it felt like he did.

Hold on...

Gatlin ducked behind a headstone barely two blocks into his journey.

Dimo.

He was spitting on the glass around Oscar's tomb, then rubbing it with his elbow. Gatlin peeked over the headstone and watched him. *Spit-rub, spit-rub... there he goes again*. He was wearing a denim jacket and after each spit, he would tug on the jacket sleeve before grinding his elbow against the glass. Gatlin stared fascinated until Dimo stopped mid-rub and answered his phone.

Felicity was out of patience and she made that clear to Dimo as soon as he cooed her name. "Twenty minutes to draw a goddamn heart and take a photo!" she said. "What's taking so long?"

"It is not working."

"What?"

"Rubbing."

She backtracked. "The erasing... the heart?"

"It is made of special stuff. I have made a hole in my jacket and my elbow is sore." Felicity pulled up the photo of the heart he'd sent earlier. No way of knowing what it was made of from that.

She looked more closely at the photo. She recalled that Oscar's tomb was on the Avenue Carette, a busy street. The FBI had left the Ferret's heart at the other end where it was less conspicuous.

"Okay... don't erase it, blank it out. Use the lipstick I gave you. Make it a red blob."

"My lipstick is pink."

She sprinted on the spot, pounding out her frustration with her feet. "That will be fine," she said finally through gritted teeth. "A pink blob is good too. And when you finish, draw a new heart in a different place, one that's easy to see, and put the numbers in like I told you. Plus—listen carefully—I want you to add an F—"

"For Ferret?"

"Exactly. Then send photos of all your work to me." She hung up and checked on Gatlin's location via her app while she was waiting for Dimo's follow-up. "Crap..." Gatlin was in the cemetery. She tried to figure out if he was within eyeshot of Dimo by cross-referencing the GPS map and the visitor's map, but it was impossible to correlate the two. So she called him.

Gatlin was more than within eyeshot. He was all but looking over the big Bulgarian's shoulder as he drew a heart and wrote numbers in it. Sneaking from one tombstone to the next, he'd ended up crouched behind a neighboring grave and poked his phone's camera lens just above the headstone, zooming in closer to complete the periscope effect. So when his phone rang, he yelped and jerked it down.

"Where the hell are you?"

It sounded like her teeth were grinding.

Gatlin glanced down at his ankle tag. Not much point in lying. And his close proximity to Dimo surely explained the hammering her tooth enamel was getting.

"In the cemetery waiting for your call."

"Where in the cemetery?"

"On my way to Jim Morrison's grave. I'm killing time. I knew you'd want me here sooner or later."

The grinding stopped, replaced by heavy breathing. Gatlin listened intently and with considerable pleasure, being of an age at which a woman panting in his ear—even on the phone—was about as good as it got.

"Okay... just stay away from the writer's tomb. There's FBI around there."

"Jim's grave is down by the main entrance. I went there when I was a lad."

"Good. That's good. Go there and hang out with the other zombies."

The insult skipped on by, but the z-word did jog his memory.

"Hey... when do I contact Mr. Z?"

"Soon. I'll send you instructions."

Gatlin hung up and slid his periscope phone over the headstone to take a peek. No sign of Dimo. He panned around, catching him in the distance heading for the exit, his big shoulders and swagger unmistakable. Gatlin stood up and went to inspect Dimo's handiwork. First, the spit-rub-scribble artwork, which turned out to be an ugly splotch, all streaks of reddish color. Gatlin rubbed at the graffiti with his fist and a heart appeared like the one he'd seen Dimo scrawl at the other end of the barrier. He went back and forth between them. So Dimo had covered up one heart and left a new one.

His phone chirped.

A photo.

Its subject was the heart he was looking at—Dimo's heart.

The Witch had told him not to go near Oscar's tomb, then sent him a photo of what Dimo had written there. Odd that. And only one explanation. The covered-up heart was her secret, and she wanted to keep it that way. But what were the numbers for? His phone rang. The answer was imminent.

"Did you get the photo?" Felicity was standing by the window, looking down at the street, waiting for Dimo. She'd told him to move his ass. With wily Wingnut sniffing around Père Lachaise, she couldn't relax until she knew he was well clear.

"Yes, ma'am, I did. I was just looking at it. What do the numbers mean?"

"Send that photo to Z. Tell him the first number is the section of the cemetery and the second is a grave number inside that section. So all he has to do is look that up. Then go there and leave a bunch of lilies with the diamonds in it."

"Why all the palaver? Why don't I just look it up and tell him?"

"The reason for the p-a-l-a-v-e-r," Felicity said in her poshest *Downton Abbey* accent, "my dearest Wingnut, is because that's what *I say*. And I'm calling the shots."

"But what if Mr. Z asks me? I can't tell him that. We were supposed to meet at Oscar's grave. Now I come up with all this malarkey. He'll smell a rat."

"Okay, I didn't want to complicate things. But you have a right to know. The FBI agent—the fake Ferret— wrote a heart with two numbers on Oscar's tomb. The idea was that there'd be no digital record, no trail. So since our plan is to rip off those diamonds, I tried to erase the FBI's heart and replace it with *our* heart. But the FBI's heart couldn't be erased. So to avoid confusion, it's best to send him a photo."

"But can't I just tell him which grave to leave the stones at?"

"Yes, you could, but I'd have no control over that process."

"But what if I say to you I've sent this photo and I lie? Instead I contact him and tell him to meet me somewhere else, or I tell him to leave the gems at a third tomb? Then I grab the loot, cut off this bracelet and make a run for it?"

"Boy... you're really thinking a lot these days, aren't you? That's a worry. But as it is, you're in line for a fifty percent share of a fortune, and I'm betting you have the brains to figure out that half of really big is still big enough to live the kind of life you dream of—an endless stream of bimbos, mountains of pot, vats of beer and whiskey and all the bangers and mash you can eat."

"Bangers and mash?"

"Or whatever that gross shit you Brits eat is called, you can feast on bucketloads."

"Sounds appealing—"

"And even if you have twice as much money, you won't be able to eat, drink, smoke or fuck any more. So what's the point? Especially as that option comes with a downside. One day, while wallowing in your preferred stupor, pending the arrival of a fresh bimbolina—*quelle surprise*—an angry witch will appear instead, she of the vengeful spirit and long memory. *Bang-bang.* I know what you're thinking, but forget it. A bullet in the brain is what you'll beg for after I make a few surgical adjustments to your manly tackle…" She sighed. "I'm getting a hard-on just thinking about it. So I'm a wee bit hopeful you'll be that stupid. But I do believe you're too much of a survivor."

"So you're trusting me?"

"You could call it that…"

"In your own sweet way… I think you've got a bit of a crush on me."

"Oh… please."

"Don't worry, I'll send the photo."

"And update me?"

"And update you."

As soon as he hung up, Gatlin studied the cemetery map, referencing the photos. The Witch had miscalculated. He was not only stupid enough to risk getting his balls rewired, but he was smart enough to figure this all out for what it was: a shell game, the short con, three shells and one pea. Only here there were three graves and one packet of diamonds. The FBI-Ferret had a grave, the Witch had a grave, and it took Gatlin less than a minute to get one too. Rothschild, a banker from way back when bankers had been heroes celebrated for their generosity, instead of crooks derided for their greed. *A banker.*

The irony of getting his big payday from a dead banker brought a smile to Gatlin's lips, although his occupation had played no part in his selection. His X factor had been the location of his tomb, adjacent to the Repos exit. Beyond it was the quiet street of the same name with the Phillipe-Auguste Metro close by. So as soon as he knew the stones were there, he could cut off the bracelet, sprint to the tomb and grab the diamonds. He'd be out of the gate in seconds. Elsewhere, the FBI would be pouncing on some poor sucker at the Victor Noir tomb, the Witch would be bellowing curses at the Edith Piaf tomb, and someone would land the unenviable job of explaining to a large oil wrestler how everything had gotten cocked up.

Whoopee!

7/61

Gatlin wrote the fateful numbers in the heart, took the photo and sent it to Zaza along with the instructions. Then he sent a message to the Witch, confirming that he'd followed through on her orders as agreed.

Felicity was at the window when she received the message, waiting to catch sight of Dimo as soon as he entered the street below.

Good news.

Or so it was on the surface. But years of living off her wits had honed her radar to an acute sensitivity...

Why was Gatlin so nice to her? Did he really believe he'd end up with half the diamonds? She'd bullied and humiliated him from day one, and he should have been properly cowed by now. But he wasn't. He was like a rubber ball that bounced back harder every time you bashed it.

She saw Dimo coming down the street, stretching his buffoon's grin to the max when he passed a slutty Parisienne in baggy culottes. The dummy actually turned and walked backwards a few steps to get the rear-end view. Felicity couldn't hear from behind the closed window, but she guessed he was hollering some obscenity. The woman didn't look back or break stride, but she did offer a one-finger salute.

Vive la France!

Felicity looked back at her phone. That interruption had cleared her head and a great idea popped into the empty space.

The photo.

If Dimo had had the location setting turned on...

She pulled up the photo he'd sent her and checked the GPS coordinates. Then she opened Gatlin's bracelet app, and... "Jim Morrison, my ass." The coordinates were identical. That bastard had been right there watching Dimo as he lied to her. She took her gun from the safe, stuck it in her bag and slammed the door behind her.

THIRTEEN

"What do you think?" Zaza showed Eve Gatlin's photo. They were sitting in a van tucked in a cul-de-sac only minutes from Père Lachaise. The van was decked out like a mobile TV news unit with walls of monitors inside and antennas on the roof.

She shook her head, looking beyond the photo at the freeze frames taken by their hidden cameras throughout the day. The big man—nicknamed Gym Bunny by Zaza—had been one of many people scribbling doodles on the glass barrier that morning, but his had assumed special interest when Gatlin had paid it so much attention. After much ado, he'd edited it, replacing it with his own version. That was the heart he'd sent them. Their hidden camera was high resolution, so they'd had no difficulty in making out the numbers before he'd changed them, and after when he'd changed them back. Now they had his instructions to decipher the numbers. But it still didn't make sense.

"From Edith Piaf to Rothschild, and back. Why the switch?"

The mystery was compounded by unknown goings-on at the other end of the tomb. Because of the close proximity of neighboring graves, Zaza had only fixed one camera. So they had no visibility of the other end of the tomb, where Gatlin and Gym Bunny had spent so much time scraping and fiddling.

"Let's take a closer look and pick up some flowers on the way," Eve said.

"And the diamonds?"

"We'll wait and see... but bring them."

They left the van and headed to the cemetery, picking up several bunches of white lilies in the Rue des Pyrénées on the way. Eve was quiet most of the way and Zaza left her in peace to think it through. He was quietly confident that she'd come to the same conclusion as he had. This was a con, a foolish enterprise that was about to reach its rightful end, the trash bin. Money and time had been lost, but the gems in his pocket had at least been saved, and on the way— praise be to Allah—his wife had joined the jihad. Soon, she would be enjoying the life of a warrior's bride with all the trimmings, like getting butt-fucked three times a day by a smelly guy with a beard and a Kalashnikov.

When they reached the tomb of the Irish writer, they stood back and watched the scene. It was only then that Zaza noticed he was holding Eve's hand.

When had that happened?

Had he done that, or had she? What the heck! It felt s-o-o-o good. Casually they approached the hidden end of the tomb where Oscar's twenty-ton rock was squeezed up against a forgotten French grave.

"My, my...," Eve said, "yet another heart and another number." She smiled up at Zaza and took her hand from his before touching the heart. "It's been stuck on... printed."

Zaza scrubbed at it with his fingernails, peeling off chunks in seconds. "You're right. And someone tried to cover it up." He waved at the smeared background of pink lipstick as she took a photo.

"And someone uncovered it."

This had to be the moment, and Zaza went for it.

"It's a con. They're even stabbing each other in the—" He broke off when a young couple stood close to them.

"Let's find a quiet spot where we can talk," Eve said.

Zaza nodded and she slid away from the glass wall and he fell in behind her. Too bad that couple had showed up. He might have closed the deal out right there. He caught up with Eve, who was checking something on her phone. He walked sedately at her side, letting her work. He'd missed his shot. But she'd come to her own conclusion in her own sweet time. She led him off the road into a labyrinth of graves belonging to the little people of Paris. No celebrities here, just butchers, bakers, and candlestick makers. They sat on a black stone that caught some shade from a nearby maple tree, and for some time they were silent, with Eve thumbing through the videos they'd shot of the tomb.

"There's no way to know for sure," she said finally.

"What?"

"Who put that stencil there. Not many people write on that side of the barrier, and this heart is very low. So they had to be sitting. That cuts out all but a few. So most likely, it was him." She showed Zaza the video of an old man with a stick. "See how calculating he is about his movements... like they've been rehearsed."

"But what does it matter... if it's a con?"

Eve left it unanswered, switching the feedback to the live camera. Zaza followed it all, getting frustrated. What was it going to take for her to smell the coffee? She zoomed in close and as she did so, Zaza saw something on the edge of the wide frame, not a face but a shape he recognized.

"Go back," he said.

She pinched back to the wide shot of visitors milling around the tomb. "There"—he pointed—"Gym Bunny. He's back and he's found himself a friend." They checked out the woman as she approached the glass barrier with the man at her side.

"That's his boss," Eve said.

"How do you know?"

"Look who's doing the talking. Besides... check the boots."

"Fancy."

"Lucchese."

"So?"

"Six thousand euros and change." Eve zoomed in closer and panned up and down on the woman as the couple stood at the barrier in front of the Gatlin-edited version of their heart. The woman was jabbing her finger at it repeatedly as she spoke. Then she aimed her finger at the man, its long, colorful nail an inch from his nose. "Fake nails, fake hair, fake tits... but great boots."

"What do you make of it?"

"It's a mess."

"Thank God we found out soon enough. If we back out now we'll—"

"No."

"Madame, please—"

"That Croatia assassination, and there were others. I told you—those details. There's no one but the Ferret and a few law enforcement types who would know that."

"Then maybe that's the answer. Law enforcement. The whole thing's a setup. Entrapment."

"You planted eight cameras. Did you see any cops, any activity that looked like an ambush being set up?" He made no answer. There'd been nothing out of the ordinary. "Besides, do these goons look like FBI to you. And since when do special agents wear six-thousand-euro boots?"

No answer to that either. So they watched in silence as Gym Bunny and Lucchese acted out their silent drama.

Closer to the scene, the drama was anything but silent. Felicity was throwing a fit, and with only Dimo available, he was getting the brunt of it. They were looking at the Ferret's heart, the one Benny's FBI cronies had supposedly posted. Someone had rubbed off Dimo's crude cover-up, someone named Gatlin, no doubt. They went back to Dimo's heart and Felicity checked it against the photo he'd sent her. The heart was the same and so were the numbers, except they weren't. They still pointed to Edith Piaf's grave, but they'd been written by another hand. Dimo's were big and bold, childlike but made with a steady hand— these were smaller and squigglier, the kind of numbers that an aging, burned-out pothead lush like Gatlin would write. So he'd erased Piaf's number, replaced it with his own, sent that photo to the money man, then switched the number back.

Now what grave was in the photo Gatlin had sent?

The two-million-dollar diamond question.

She checked the GPS bracelet app. Gatlin was on the move. He wouldn't take the GPS bracelet off until he was ready to make the pickup at whatever grave he'd sent them to and he was sure to shed it, like a snake its skin, a long way from where he was likely to be. She had to find him before then, drag him behind a tombstone and crack his head open against it. As she turned away from the phone, it buzzed a cryptic message from Benny, a single character...

?

He was no doubt getting antsy as he'd heard nothing. Too bad. Gatlin was the priority. He could dump that bracelet at any moment. She started off, heading towards Gatlin's beep, but second thoughts pulled her up sharp. If she didn't answer Benny immediately, he'd call her, and in her current mood who knew where that conversation would end up? *Fob him off*. It was the only choice, keep him sweet for just a little longer...

She thumbed in a message at hyperspeed.

All done. Waiting for drop-off. Will revert soonest.

Nice touch, adding the word *revert*. It sounded so professional. She'd picked it up temping at a law firm back in her drama school days before she'd traded a keyboard for a single-tailed whip. With Benny quieted, at least temporarily, she strode off, one hand holding her phone, her eyes on Gatlin's beep, the other tucked in her bag, her finger curling around the trigger of her Colt Cobra.

Eve and Zaza watched Lucchese & Co. leave the camera's field of vision. Then Eve backed out of the camera app and brought up the photo of the old man's heart.

92/50

She checked it against her map listing the location of celebrity tombs.

"Victor Noir—killed by an assassin."

She read a lot into that discovery and it showed in her smile.

"You still want to go ahead with this?" Zaza said, dumbfounded.

She let the question hang there as she backed up the recording, navigating to the old man section and advancing it frame by frame. Because of the foot traffic around the busy tomb, the old man was only visible in a few frames, and it was in the last of these, as he walked away, that she found it, zooming in on his right hand as it swung back behind his body. The pixels were stretched, the image fuzzy, but the bottom of a heart on the palm of his hand was unmistakable.

"Son of a bitch"—she pointed at her phone—"the old man who barely touched the barrier. One hand. Just enough to transfer some high-tech stencil. That's exactly what the world's top assassin would do. I'll give you odds-on this nobody is the Ferret."

Zaza stared at the image, hope fading. "But how do you explain these other hearts and the—?"

"Lucchese is linked to the Ferret and she was planning to rip him off. But the way he set it up made that impossible. So she had to improvise."

"And Mr. G?"

"Bit of a mystery. I'd have said Lucchese's partner, but with that bracelet, he's most likely a gofer on probation who's in business for himself."

Zaza gave up. She was right. That was the hell of it.

"The lilies..." She pointed to the bunch under his arm. "We'll make three bunches. The one with the diamonds we'll leave at the Victor Noir tomb along with a camera. You still have one left?"

"Several."

"And before we do that, we'll drop off the other two empty bouquets."

"Why?"

"Consolation prizes. To show we're not the idiots they take us for. Then message Mr. G, as arranged... and won't he get a surprise."

They checked all around for eyes. No one. And set to work on the flowers.

Gatlin was thinking about Julie Andrews. He often daydreamed about encounters with famous actresses, so nothing new there, although Ms. Andrews had never made the cut to date and would frankly have been poorly cast in most of them. But this was a different type of dream. No age restrictions or content-warning labels required. Indeed, it was less of a dream than an out-of-body experience... *the hills are alive with the sound of music*... Gatlin Fry knew the feeling. It had glowed out of her as she'd run through the alpine flowers and now it belonged to him.

Yessiree... this might be billed as The Day of the Ferret... but it's my day.

Gatlin pumped his fists as if pummeling an opponent in a clinch. Then he continued more sedately, reining it all in. The jewels were not in his hands yet. Things could go wrong, although that seemed unlikely. All he had to do was get the bolt cutter, and...

He stopped. What if the bastards had found it? What if they'd been laying a trail of newbie ashes and the machine had snagged on it? No more running through alpine flowers. Gatlin set off at an angst-driven sprint, heading towards the green hill behind the crematorium.

FOURTEEN

With his hands on the bolt cutter, Gatlin snuck off out of sight. It was the joy of a cemetery. So many places to sneak. He fitted the blades of the bolt cutter around the bracelet, jammed a handle between the tombstone and the ground, then dropped his ass on the other handle.

All things considered, it went well. The bracelet popped off, and that was the important part. The incidentals—the handle slipping off his ass and jamming up his butt crack to an unimaginable depth— were judged to be an acceptable cost to pay, and if truth be told, the best sex he'd had in a long while.

He peeked over the tombstone. There had been a squeal-like-a-pig moment when the bolt cutter had engaged him in that unlawful public act and he was anxious not to draw attention to himself. Now he'd cut the umbilicus between him and the Witch, she'd surely hunt him down. He remembered the pistol she'd brandished in Benidorm and had no doubt that she'd use it if crossed, and crossed she had been.

Gatlin jumped up. She'd be on the way already. He hurled the bracelet as far as he could, noting with satisfaction that it landed in a clump of bushes between graves. That would burn up a good bit of her time. Enough anyway. A message from Zaza to say the diamonds were at the grave might already be zinging its way across the airways, and if not, it would be sometime soon. He checked his map and headed towards the Rothschild tomb, picking his way through the graves. The cross-country route was shorter and cut the risk of a chance encounter with the Witch, although it did take longer with so many tombs to circumnavigate. So Gatlin made haste, chuckling as he scampered from grave to grave.

James baron de Rothschild... get out your checkbook, mate!

His circuitous routing paid off and he arrived without incident. But what a letdown! No white lilies. He shuffled off behind the grave, finding a secluded spot where he could wait undisturbed and unseen until the message came from Z. Then it would all be down to a quick... *one-two*. Grab the lilies and exit via the nearby Repos Gate, never to be seen again. He sat on a grave with his back to a weatherworn headstone. The sun had been in and out of clouds all day and he'd picked the perfect *out* moment to catch a few rays. His head rocked back against the stone, mind rambling over the day's events and the morrow's prospects. No dozing, you understand. Gatlin was nobody's fool. Hadn't he eschewed the sacred weed and sworn off the devil's brew to guarantee this bristling alertness? Yes, his eyelids did close, but that was only to block the sun. Behind them, like a vigilant sentry, his senses were primed to catch the slightest sound out of the ordinary, the merest scent of...

What's that?

Gatlin sniffed again, harder. And his eyes popped open.

No second-guessing that fragrance.

He scrambled up onto his knees before sucking down a deep lungful.

Yes... no doubt.

He spun his head around, seeking its origin.

Who's got that doobie?

He sprang up, then remembered the pistol-packing Witch in hot pursuit and ducked back down. He took a peek more warily—there was nobody in sight—and sniffed in a few long breaths. Lovely stuff. Sweet and spicy, but with a tarry aftertaste. He checked his map again.

Section six, tomb forty-six... the Jim Morrison tomb.

It had to be coming from there. The Rothschild memorial was in section seven, right next door, and Jim's section six was upwind. He could easily nip over there, cadge a hit and be back on sentry duty within minutes. There was nothing happening here in any case, and although the armor-plated guarantees he'd added to his sobriety pledge were an obstacle, it was not insurmountable with Boris Johnson's groundbreaking *Zen and the Art of Weasel Hole Maintenance* offering characteristically no-nonsense advice for dealing with agreements that had outgrown their usefulness.

Shredding machine.

Therefore, with the tacit approval of the wannabe UK prime minister, Gatlin sneaked around tombs, heading towards... he stopped, a horrid thought pulling him up sharp.

Jim Morrison?

He'd been on his way to Jim's grave that morning when the Witch had called and he'd been dumb enough to blurt out his destination to cover up his spying on Dimo.

What to do?

He'd pulled the plug on the bracelet now. There was no going back on that. The Witch was hunting him for sure. But where would she look? Her first choice had to be Jim's tomb. He sat down grumpily to consider the matter, his thinking soon bent out of shape by the smoke-stained breeze, its siren scent sucking him towards doom. Yes, he had mentioned the Jim Morrison tomb. But all it took was a quick round of mental gymnastics for that to be viewed in a positive light. Surely that would be the last place she'd check. She'd know he'd never be stupid enough to go to a place he'd actually told her about.

That was a fine judgment call...

How stupid am I versus how stupid she thinks I am...?

It was a tricky debate and he concluded that he was too stupid to figure it out properly, so he gave up and pressed on with the mission, darting across roads and navigating section five with extreme caution.

Jim's grave was busy. But no sign of the Witch. Gatlin scouted it before approaching a young couple he'd determined to be the source of his lure. They were sitting on a curb nearby, sharing a big doobie and mumbling about its quality. The boy was in jeans, but the girl was wearing a summery dress and she had a bouquet of crumpled flowers in her lap that looked like they'd been harvested locally. Their tousled long hair completed the picture. Americans. Gatlin would recognize that stoned mumbling anywhere.

"Greetings," he said. "You look so sweet. You remind me of me and my late wife when we were kids. Too bad I don't have any decent weed to offer you. Then you wouldn't have to smoke that crap you're toking."

"Oh no, man... you got that wrong," the boy said. "We got this in Amsterdam. This weed's the terminator—"

"It's grown-under-lights crap. You should have seen the stuff we grew in the Hindu-Kush, let me tell you—"

"Take a hit." The boy offered up the joint. "See for yourself."

Gatlin shook his head. "I couldn't. I—"

"Do it, Grandpa," the girl said. "It's the bomb."

Gatlin looked down at her, startled.

Grandpa?!

She looked like the heroine in a zombie porn movie, the whites of her eyes a latticework of red.

"Just to be social." Gatlin took the joint, waving his other hand for them to make room so he could sit on the curb between them. He took a long hit as he did so, murmuring, not an actual word, not dismissive or approving, just pondering. This was a tasting session that was evidently going to take some time. And so Gatlin sucked away at the joint while the young Americans stared in bug-eyed wonderment. Maybe it was the length of his tokes that fascinated them, or maybe it was the length of time he held the smoke in his lungs, his cheeks bulging and his eyes rolling. When he finally passed the joint on to the girl, it was a sodden wisp of paper so small she had to pinch it with her nails to hold it.

"I see what you mean," Gatlin said after clearing his lungs with a spectacular coughing fit. "It's not bad." He got to his feet. "But you should have smoked that..." He abandoned whatever was left of his sentence and wandered off as though the Americans had never existed and nor had the Witch. And on that latter point, he got lucky as he made tentative steps like a baby who'd just discovered what his legs can do. He felt comfortable, not troubled by anything, his head a vacant lot unencumbered with stuff, although there was something scratching to get in, some thought, some...

Rothschild... diamonds, Mr. Z... the Witch.

Gatlin stumbled off the road in panic, ducking behind the first big gravestone he could find.

What's going on?

Pot had never affected him like this.

Just need a minute to...

And maybe it was a minute, maybe a lot more. Eventually, Gatlin stood up, the ground under his feet oddly spongy, and checked the cemetery map on his phone. Just a bit of cross-country dodging in and out of tombs and he'd be back at his sentry post waiting for Zaza. Strange about the map, though... how some of the graves had moved since the last time he'd looked. He stuck his phone back in his pocket. He'd go with the force. It had always worked before. He set off, but after a few steps something happened. Exactly what was unclear. Something involving him and the ground. Maybe it was a trip, catching his foot on a tombstone, or a stumble as he stepped onto the wonky turf. Whatever it was, Gatlin dived like a swimmer setting off on a freestyle sprint.

When he came to, he was somewhere else, and his ass was sore as if he'd been dragged over stony ground and a few gravestones on the way to this unknown location.

"We missed you... didn't we, Dimo?" Gatlin looked from the Witch to the grinning hunk at her side and back, his head woozy, his mind scrambling to fill in the gap since he'd gone looking for a hit off a joint. "It's going to be wonderfully theatrical." She continued. "Your screaming as we torture you here amongst the tombs."

"Screaming... why?"

"Because we're torturing you, silly."

"Yeah... but why?"

"Where's the bracelet?"

"It fell off."

The Witch cuffed him, snapping his head to the side, her titanium nails gouging streaks of red in his cheek.

"We know you reassigned the drop spot. So just tell me where and I might let you live." She pulled out her shiny gun and fitted his nose into the end of the barrel.

"If you shoot me, you'll never know."

"You're right." She put the gun away in her bag, taking out a switchblade knife instead. "Did you see *Chinatown*?" She stuck the blade under his nose. "That part where Roman Polanski goes—" Gatlin's phone rang and three sets of eyeballs swiveled down to his pocket. "Now why didn't I think of that?" She took the phone out and held it up in front of his face, but that didn't work. "You smartass... you disabled the face recognition. So what's the PIN?"

Gatlin composed himself, enjoying the moment, a minor victory after that whack in the face.

"In the time it'll take you to torture it out of me, someone could steal those lilies. Why risk losing everything? There's enough money there for all three of us. If we're really partners, I'll tell you right now, and we can go and get it together. But you must promise."

"We were already partners... until you cut that bracelet off."

"You were going to double-cross me."

For a moment, it looked like she was going to argue the point, but then she moved on.

"I promise I won't double-cross you," she said.

"And him?"

"Tell him, Dimo."

"Sure. No tricks. Three-way split."

Gatlin looked back and forth between them, eyes narrowing.

"Pinky promise?" he said, offering up a loose fist, his little finger poking out invitingly.

The Witch snorted with impatience, but she locked pinkies and they shook. A bewildered Dimo followed suit when elbowed into action by his boss. The ritual done, Gatlin struggled to his feet. "Here, give me the phone." He reached for it, still wobbly. "I'll see what he says..." She handed it over with obvious reluctance, giving Dimo the on-guard nod. Gatlin shook his head as if clearing it as Dimo stepped behind him and put one hand on his shoulder.

"Thanks, mate," Gatlin said. "I'm still finding my legs and that's a big help." He fumbled with his phone, mumbling to himself. "That stuff! What are those kids smoking? It should be illegal." He tapped in a PIN but it was rejected. "Wait... wait, I got it." He tried again and the screen opened up. He smiled at the Witch as he looked up. But then he snapped his head back, crunching Dimo in the face. The big man stumbled back, catching his foot on a neighboring tomb and keeling over. The Witch dived into her bag, but Gatlin body-checked her, sending her reeling backwards and tripping as she pulled out her gun. Gatlin heard the shot as he darted away, dodging between tombs, his head as clear as the first dawn.

The lilies?

Could they still be there? Based on past experience, Gatlin wasn't hopeful. He was going through the motions, of course. But then again, he always did. He'd always had a plan and he'd always seen it through. He wasn't a quitter—a loser maybe, but not a quitter. That was his karma. His was the journey, not the destination. It had always been like that.

Except today...

There they were, the lilies, leaning against the Rothschild grave. He snatched them up. People were milling around, startled people, staring wide-eyed. Maybe it was the way he'd run up and snatched the flowers.

But no... they're not looking at me. They're looking at...

Gatlin saw her just in time, ducking as her first shot hacked a chunk out of the banker's tombstone. He spun off behind it and cowered there before clutching his lilies to his breast and breaking cover.

The Repos Gate was just a few yards away. If he could only get... but the Witch was too close. She'd be out on the street behind him within seconds. The Rue du Repos was a narrow one-way street with stone walls on one side and buildings on the other. It was a perfect shooting gallery. She'd be able to take her time and nail his ass. The cemetery was a better bet—chunks of rock everywhere, trees, bushes, and plenty of people with phones to video a crazy American running amok with a gun.

It was a touch-and-go choice until a group of Japanese tourists marched into view, heading for a nearby toilet. There was already a line there. So the two converging groups offered plenty of human shields. Gatlin went for the gap between them with shots zinging out behind him. Dodging side to side, he stumbled, dropping the lilies, and as he stooped to pick them up, they exploded in a shower of broken stems, and shards of flint and sparks. But no diamonds.

Gatlin looked back at the Witch. She couldn't have been aiming at the lilies. She couldn't be that good a shot, or he'd be dead already, a conclusion she had no doubt reached herself as she was in a combat stance, both hands on the gun taking careful aim. He jumped to the side as she fired, making it across the avenue and hiding behind a tomb in section four. There was a bush next to the grave, and he could see through its sparse foliage, giving him a good view of the chaos he'd left in his wake.

The people waiting outside the toilets were gone, doubtless now packed five to a cubicle and making new friends fast. Oddly, the Japanese tourists hadn't moved. They were all videoing the performance with their phones aimed at the Witch, perhaps believing it was all a theme park event put on for their benefit. She was no longer running, barely sauntering, the gun hanging at her hip.

The tourists parted in waves as she approached the section where Gatlin had hidden. Clearly, she'd lost him. She seemed to notice her audience for the first time. She put the gun in her bag and waved to them and they all waved back, with some of the more traditional types adding a bow. Then she looked beyond the tourists up the avenue and whatever she saw there froze her to the spot for a moment. Then she turned and sprinted for the exit. The tour group hooted and clapped, the staged gunfight a runaway hit, and plenty of five-star reviews heading the way of Père Lachaise. When the Witch had disappeared through the gate, Gatlin emerged from his hiding place.

What had she seen?

He looked up the avenue. It ran as far as the Monument of the Dead, a rambling sculpture much favored by visitors as a backdrop for selfies. Not anymore. Now its visitors were all pointing their phones in the opposite direction, catching the aftermath of the shoot-out as uniforms ran towards the action. Gatlin crept off to find a quiet tomb, not to cry. His plan hadn't worked, but no tears about that. They never did. What he needed was somewhere to figure out the mystery of why it had failed. He stretched himself out on a handsome slab of marble and peered up through branches at rivers of blue between puffs of white cloud.

Could he have picked up the wrong bunch of flowers?

No... it couldn't be that. There were no other lilies on the grave. In fact, there were no other flowers at all. Rothschild was a banker, not a rock star or a poet.

Had they left the diamond lilies somewhere else?

At the Witch's Edith Piaf tomb?

But if they'd left the diamonds there, why was the Witch chasing him? There was only one plausible answer. They'd seen through the scam. And that empty bunch of lilies blown into compost by the angry Witch was their thumb-on-the-nose rebuke. But they'd outsmarted themselves. Stealing those diamonds was doing them a favor. As they'd soon realize when they showed up at the Victor Noir tomb and the FBI pounced on them. Maybe it had already happened. Gatlin set off, picking a route through the graves. If not, he should get there just in time to enjoy the fireworks.

FIFTEEN

Peering up the avenue towards the Monument of the Dead, if Gatlin had looked more closely, he might have noticed a striking couple in the crowd, a man and a woman looking his way, the man built square, a monument in his own right, the woman slender like one of those lilies the Witch had pulverized with her thirty-eight.

"Jackpot," Eve said.

Zaza nodded somberly. They'd been heading to Victor Noir's grave with the last of the lilies and all of the diamonds when they'd heard shots and turned to see Gatlin's frenzied appearance at the other end of the avenue, followed by Lucchese's Annie Oakley routine and Gatlin's disappearance into the labyrinth of tombs. So Zaza's hope for a last-minute bolthole out of this madness—was fading fast. Now all they had to do was leave the flowers and get the hell out before the Ferret got there. Zaza discounted any possibility of Gatlin actually communicating the location to the Ferret. But the old man who'd left that message by leaning on the glass was clearly not to be underestimated. He was sure to be back and might have eyes on them leaving the package.

On arrival at Noir's tomb, they waited until its only other visitor, an elderly woman in a studded-leather vest and denim jeans, had finished her ritual, a curious mélange of Hail Marys and bronze penis stroking. Then they left the flowers. It was like an out-of-body experience for Zaza, his world a dreamscape with him driving off a cliff in slow motion. He didn't want to do it, but he couldn't take his hands off the wheel.

On Eve's instructions, Zaza removed some withered stalks from the top hat held in Victor Noir's right hand and replaced them with the lilies. When they were done, they stood respectfully, heads lowered as if in prayer. Then Eve checked her camera app. They'd already mounted a tiny spy cam on a low-traffic tomb nearby. Zaza peeked over her shoulder at the screen. The camera was doing its job. They'd know who ended up with the diamonds. Zaza slipped his arm around her.

"We'd better get out of here," he said.

As Zaza and Eve went looking for a quiet spot to bide their time, Benny Capone was enjoying exactly that. He was lounging in his recliner in the humidor of his Manhattan apartment and sucking on an Hoyo de Monterrey, Double Corona from his special stock, imported back in the Obama years when restrictions on Cuban trade had been loosened up, only to be reinstated by the current, and soon-to-be-deceased, president.

He sucked on his cigar with that happy thought in mind. After that phone call, he'd fled from his office, and he'd been holed up in his apartment ever since, monitoring the president's tweets for any mention of his sacking. It hadn't been made official. After all, he wasn't an appointee. He was just a lawyer who'd been dropped. Rump had to be itching to trash him, but he'd hold off. If word got around that his wife had played around, his macho reputation would be in the dirt.

Besides, with the D-Day trip imminent, he'd been too busy having Europhobic panic attacks.

On a previous trip, a baby-Rump blimp had stalked him in the UK, and on his return he'd suffered flashbacks symptomatic of PTSD. It had gotten so bad they'd hired the former UK premier Tony Blair—for a reputed eight-figure fee—to give him counseling. Spinmeister Blair, best known for dragging Britain into Iraq after getting snarled up in Dubya's coattails while kissing his ass, had argued that Rump's European policy of "tough love" was a triumph of diplomacy. According to the *Blair Analysis*, by hitting America's allies with punitive tariffs and undermining their democracies, the canny leader of the free world was actioning a masterful strategy. After thousands of years of internecine warfare, Rump had forged the fractious Europeans into a unified whole. At last, this squabbling polyglot horde agreed on something. They hated him, especially the ones who had to make nice to get their US handouts. The John Thomas loved it, soaking up Blair's dizzying spin so thoroughly that he was soon crowing on social media that:

MY unpresidented diplomacy gifts lasting peach to Europe

Despite all that, he'd had a relapse, triggered by the prospect of facing all the haters at the same time. There had even been talk of canceling the trip. But according to his latest tweet, Rump was now on his way to Air Force One, soon to be heading to Europe, never to return. Benny was already living the days after his assassination. He could see it all in a series of snapshots: the president's shattered wife deplaning, her tears streaking behind a black veil, a thick one in case a smile broke through. He'd be there for her, the family's trusted lawyer, the friend and confidant of the late president—

His Ferret phone buzzed and he snatched it up, his feelgood moment trashed by the reminder that the Bronx bitch in Paris had still not *reverted* as she'd promised, and this had to be the anxious assassin waiting for his diamonds.

Sure enough...

Delivery?

So what was he supposed to say? At such moments—Benny had learned from his distinguished career both as a lawyer and politician—it was best to be bold and bullshit.

Delivery has been actioned.

He picked up his other phone. He had no choice about it now and called the Witch, gritted teeth at the ready.

She answered the phone with, "I thought you said no calling. Encrypted texts only."

"Except in emergencies." Benny fought to get a grip. "And why are you panting? What's going on?"

"Job's done. I'm just killing time at the gym—"

"Are you bullshitting me? The gym? Your file might be at the bottom of the prosecutor's pile now, but one call from me and—"

"Hey, Benny... what's the problem? Is the FBI there? It should all be over by now."

He had to be careful here. Felicity was nobody's fool. He had to stick to the script: the FBI, the entrapment. The thought gave him pause for other reasons too. After the president had been assassinated, what would that smart brain of hers be figuring out?

The Ferret was real. Benny had to be a part of it.

That made her a liability. That file he had on her wouldn't be worth shit. She'd get immunity and testify against him. At the very least, she'd blackmail his ass, or run scared, turning into a time bomb capable of going off at any moment. There was only one answer. Get rid of her. His dad wouldn't have hesitated. Everyone knew that Angelo "Angel" Capone had busted noses and legs, but Benny knew his dad's work for the mob went a lot further than that. But all that was in the past. Benny was a lawyer, an officer of the court. He kicked Felicity's fate down the road, getting back to today's problem.

"Did the message get through to Coronata?"

"Unless that sleazeball Brit you set me up with—"

"If you took those diamonds, there's no place on Earth you—"

"No diamonds? How do you know that? The FBI check it already?"

"They say there's nothing going on at that tomb. No flowers, no nothing. Why don't you wander on by and take a look?"

"And get arrested by the FBI?"

"No, you won't, just..." A happy thought occurred. "What about the cousin of the tsar of Bulgaria? Send him."

"Okay, I can do that. I'll figure out something and get back to you."

Felicity hung up. She was huddling out of view, sitting on basement steps off some grimy backstreet. She'd escaped her pursuers. She was pretty sure of that, but she'd had to run like hell. Sending Dimo to scout around wasn't a bad idea, assuming he'd come back to life. The last she'd seen of him, he'd been lying motionless after headbutting a tombstone. That shooting spree had been plain crazy. She'd lost it. Pure and simple. But who'd have thought it? Gatlin Fry had conned her. All that whining about being partners... then that pinky promise shit. That was a masterstroke! He'd played the idiot—totally convincingly, needless to say. The cunning bastard had suckered her, then rolled the pair of them. Who'd have thought he had the balls? Still, he didn't have the diamonds. But they had to be somewhere. If not at another grave, then in someone's pocket. That big Turk's, perhaps. There was no way she could go back to that cemetery after blowing chunks out of half a dozen tombstones and starring in an online movie that had no doubt clocked up millions of views already. Thank God no one had been hit, one of the benefits of being too mad to aim straight.

She dialed Dimo. Too bad she'd told him about the FBI sting. Was he stupid enough to go poking around there and risk it?

"You okay, sweetie?" she said on hearing his woozy voice. Hopefully that smack on the head had knocked all that FBI talk into some dark recess where it was no longer accessible. "I was so worried about you."

"He escape?"

"I did my best. But I'm only a woman."

"He have the diamonds?"

"I don't know. I shot my gun a few times so—"

"In the cemetery?"

"I forgot I was in Europe."

"So what I do?"

"Find him. Or that big Turk. Check the other graves and find whoever's got those diamonds and bring them to me. Then we'll leave."

"Tonight?"

"As soon as you get the diamonds. Maybe they're at the shiny-dick grave."

"But wasn't that the... eh...?"

Felicity waited. Three letters. FBI—would he remember them and connect the dots? Tick-tock. She ran out of patience.

"When you get back, I'll do that number six thing on you."

"You got new batteries?"

"Copper-top. We're good to go."

Zaza was sitting next to Eve on a weathered white crypt, following the action at Victor Noir's tomb on her phone via their hidden camera.

For days, he had been spiraling in a whirlpool, sucked towards a vortex promising to spit him out in the balmy waters of Guantanamo Bay. Despite that, he'd always felt escape was close at hand. He was smart and strong. There'd be a moment and he'd seize it. But it hadn't showed, and now he was looking at the old man who'd left the heart on the wall walk away with a bunch of lilies containing a fortune in diamonds. The deal was done. Eve had outsmarted the con artists and outreasoned him. He was now a conspirator in an assassination plot against the US president, and if the Ferret was the equal of his reputation, John Thomas was as good as dead. Soon the Ferret would disappear from view and his last chance to stop this madness would be gone. He was about to leap up and chase through the graves and bring him down while there was still a chance. It would cost him his job, but...

Eve jerked the phone up close as another highly recognizable character came into view, taking stealthy strides in the old man's wake.

"Mr. G," Zaza said, unable to keep the smile out of his voice.

G's stride became a trot as the Ferret disappeared from view and Gatlin dived headlong... Eve tried to zoom more, but she'd already maxed it out. Whatever was going down now, it was off camera. She grabbed a handful of her hair and screeched, "Get him. Find him. Stop him."

Fifty years before, on a sodden green field under a leaden sky hemmed in on all sides by asbestos prefabs, Gatlin had made his last rugby tackle and broken a rib in the process. The coach, maintaining strict adherence to the health-and-safety rules of his day, had insisted he see out the match. After a layoff like that, it was a big ask, but two million in diamonds was all the answer he needed.

Gatlin's shoulder thundered against the back of the old man's legs and his arms locked around his thighs and down he went, the man's heel jamming between the gravel and the rib he'd busted all those years before. He yelped as the old pain met the new, and his arms fell aside long enough for the Ferret to squirm out of his grip and twist around, reaching into his jacket as Gatlin crawled up on him and grabbed his throat. But Gatlin couldn't get a grip and his hands kept slipping as the Ferret whipped out his gun.

Gatlin grabbed his wrist and jerked the gun aside as it went off. It was a lot easier than he'd expected. The Ferret wasn't very strong. Maybe it wasn't a disguise. Maybe he really was that old. Struggling for the gun, they rolled twice with Gatlin ending up on top. He still had a tight hold on the Ferret's gun arm, but his other arm was locked up by his adversary. A stalemate. Only one thing left in his arsenal: the Liverpool kiss. Gatlin tucked his chin in and smacked his forehead down on the Ferret's nose. The old man screeched—a rather effeminate screech, Gatlin noted—and grabbed his face, letting the gun fall away to the side. Gatlin was aghast. The damage he'd done with that headbutt was unreal. The old man was howling and groping at his bloody face, fingering it as if trying to stick wads of flesh back in place. For a moment, Gatlin was bordering on sympathetic, the Ferret's recent gunshot that had so nearly provided him with a cheap alternative to cosmetic ear surgery forgotten. This poor old chap looked like he'd been savaged by a pit bull. It was only then that Gatlin noticed the lilies. The bunch had been broken apart in the fracas and flowers strewn on the path ahead and lying amongst them the package of—

Gatlin leapt for the diamonds as the old man struggled up. Only he didn't struggle. His leap was better than Gatlin's, especially as it was undertaken with one hand holding his face on. Gatlin snatched up the diamonds and dived over a tombstone as the old man reached his gun, landing on a pile of dirt.

No more shots.

Gatlin kissed the packet of diamonds. He so wanted to open it. But now was clearly not the time. He snuck a peek over the tombstone instead. The Ferret was running, almost out of sight, then he was gone.

Gatlin stood up, and he was looking down at the broken lilies lying in the gravel when he noticed an eye staring back at him. He stepped closer. No wonder there'd been so much blood. He'd ripped out the Ferret's eyeball. There it was, lying amongst the lilies, only... he bent over and peered even closer. It wasn't an eye. It was a super big contact lens with a brown iris. He thought back to when he'd stared at the damage he'd done, the old man holding his face, blood soaking down from his nose, and yes... one brown eye and one blue one. That was it. He hadn't ripped anyone's face off—what he'd taken as skin was silicon, a hyper-mask, so stunningly realistic it was undetectable even at arm's length. The cracked nose had exposed it. With the bones underneath it reorganized and slicked up with blood, the mask had slipped. And that nimble movement, that sudden shift of gears, that wasn't an old man. That had to be a young man, except... a young man wouldn't have been so easy for an old man to overpower, and what about that soprano screech? Outside a few famous singers, not the sort of sound a man can produce unless his nuts are in a ringer.

Was that old man a woman?

If so, no woman would go through all that prosthetic treatment to run an errand for the Ferret. In a flash, Gatlin knew more about this feared assassin than anyone else on the planet. He'd thought he was tackling some gofer like himself who'd been assigned the task. Following some sixth sense, his eyes flashed up.

Dimo... a hundred yards off and running fast.

Too bad he hadn't had time to get the gun. But at least he had the diamonds. Gatlin dodged off between tombs. There was no way he was going to outrun Dimo, and with not enough time to hide the gems, Gatlin raced towards his only hope, the crematorium, the sanctuary of the dead.

SIXTEEN

Look good, Zaza told himself as he bounded between graves. Eve would catch him on camera as he reached the Victor Noir tomb and it had to look like he was on board with the plan. He'd almost blown it when Gatlin had appeared and launched himself at the old man. Pumping his fist and hollering *way to go* would not have been well received by his boss. If Gatlin had ended up with the diamonds, the deal would fall apart. No money, no assassination. Even if Eve was prepared to stump up more loot, the delay would surely make the current plan unworkable and give him time to talk some sense into her.

His phone buzzed a message.

Gym Bunny in hot pursuit of G! Heading NW on traversale. Saw injured old man on a gate cam. Am in hot pursuit.

He stared at those last words... hot pursuit! Was she kidding? She was chasing down an assassin, or at least his bag man. He couldn't let that happen. He'd forget G and head towards... *where?* She'd said gate, but not which one, and even if he knew, it wouldn't help. She could be anywhere by now. The only thing he could do was follow through on the task she'd assigned him and hope for the best. Zaza sprinted off—not a pretty sight—heading towards the Traversale. When he reached the crematorium, he got his first glimpse of his quarry as G disappeared behind the building with Gym

Bunny in close pursuit. Zaza reached the corner and stopped, panting. Gym Bunny was standing by steps leading down to a basement door, his eyes shifting from the door to the general area around it. As Zaza watched, he started down the steps and Zaza called out, "Hey...," and strode toward him.

Gym Bunny went back up the steps, grinning through clenched teeth. At the top of the steps, he stopped, put his hands on his hips and said, "Hello, turkey man." He flapped his elbows and shuffled his feet, kicking up dirt. "It's Thanksgiving time..."

Zaza faked a laugh. "Thanks for the entertainment," he said. "Much appreciated. But you'd better go home now and forget about this man you're chasing."

Zaza was off camera now. So he could play this one any which way he wanted. But that was the problem. He didn't know which way was best. Either of these parties ending up with the big money was fine by him. So long as it didn't get routed back to the assassin. But the only way to figure that out was to find G and have another friendly chat. That made Gym Bunny here a complication.

The man stopped his turkey dance and scowled.

"Back off, fat boy. I was the junior MMA champion of Bulgaria. You have no idea how bad this is going to be for you. Back off now, and maybe I let you live."

Zaza took a step closer and Gym Bunny lashed out a roundhouse kick aimed at his head. Zaza jammed it and scooped the leg up under his arm.

"Big mistake, turkey man. But thanks for giving me the chance to—" He hopped on his other leg, then flashed it up at Zaza's face. But he caught that one too, tucking it under his other arm. Gym Bunny snorted, then curled up his body, bringing his face up to Zaza's.

It was an impressive feat of strength, Zaza had to admit. As if acknowledging the observation, Gym Bunny tapped his taut six-pack. "Two hundred and seventy-eight—my fiancée is witness."

"Two hundred and seventy-eight what?"

Gym Bunny went to demonstrate something with his hands but then seemed to run out of patience.

"Enough fun and games," he said, making a fist and pointing at it. "Say goodnight, turkey man."

He wasn't the only one whose patience had run out. Zaza's neck muscles pinged like taut ropes as he jerked his head forward and bit his nose off, and as Gym Bunny screamed and grabbed his face, Zaza spun on the spot, using him as a counterweight. After a few spins, Zaza was about to let him go but changed his mind. The man could really damage himself and there was no need for that. He'd already been—

At this point, fate and physics intervened and Gym Bunny flew through the air and crashed into the wall. Zaza looked from side to side, noting the man's sneakers still jammed in his armpits. They were fine sneakers too, fluorescent lime green and black, only now they were empty. He arranged them reverentially next to the pile of muscles crunched at the foot of the wall, then made his way down the steps to the door that had so interested him.

As soon as Gatlin heard Dimo's voice outside the door, he ran into the room he'd blundered into the day before, recalling its assortment of empty coffins and thinking he could hide in one. Thankfully, there were no workers there today either, although they'd been busy in the meantime as all the coffins were gone, all except one. It was huge—pricey, no doubt—and made of some exquisitely grained wood. His attention went back to the corridor. He could hear movement out there and voices, and none of them happy sounding. Gatlin went to the coffin. He tried to lift the lid, but it was nailed or screwed or… no, there was a latch. Evidently, coffin lids weren't screwed on anymore. Vampire and zombie threats notwithstanding, these days the dead were merely restrained by a latch that the wimpiest of undead would have no trouble busting. He flipped it open and lifted the lid. He might have noticed a paper seal ripping too had it not been for the sight of its occupant, a middle-aged lady so big she was a wall-to-wall fit in its leather-lined luxury.

Oh no…

She had one eye open. Gatlin tried to look away, but his eyes just swiveled in their sockets, unable to break her gaze. Poor lady, he thought. *Chantal.* Her name was embroidered on the lush lining of the lid. She had to have paid a fortune for all this, and those incompetent French couldn't even shut both eyes. Gatlin wanted to do it. It seemed only right. But the sound of doors opening much closer interrupted his thoughts. Loud voices… something going on.

Hide the gems on Chantal!

What a brilliant idea! He was trapped. Dimo was certain to find him if he checked every room. But what if he said he'd hidden the gems out in the cemetery and he was happy to show him where? Once outside, he'd trip him or sucker punch him and escape. Dimo would certainly disbelieve that story and search the room. But surely he wouldn't be uncouth enough to disturb a dead person. Gatlin looked down at the woman, her long black hair radiating across the white satin pillow. Very artistic. He hadn't noticed that before, what with that lone eyeball staring at him. He had to close that. There was no hiding anything on her while she was eyeballing him. If he could only get past that eye, he could tuck the diamonds under the pillow. He took a deep breath, the whiff of embalming fluid giving his heart a jolt and sending his head spinning. He slid his fingers around her wrist, being careful to keep his hands on the silk of her gown and avoid touching her skin.

Another door opened, much closer, loud voices.

He was running out of time. Gatlin lifted her hand up towards her face. Three of her fingers were curled, but her index finger with a long red nail at the end was pointed. He hooked the nail on the eyelid and tried to drag it down over the eye. But he couldn't get any leverage on it because of her floppy wrist. The only way this was going to work was if he held the finger directly, and if he was going to touch her finger, he might as well touch her eyelid and be done with it. So he kept trying until a deep, horribly familiar voice boomed from somewhere very close to the other side of that door.

"Gatlin… I just want to talk."

Zaza!

Gatlin heard French voices too, a clamor raised in protest, but Zaza was ignoring them. The Turk's bone-crunching demo in Benidorm flashed through his head, prompting a wave of panic, and he fumbled his handiwork, snagging on Chantal's fake eyelash and dragging it to her lip, where it sat like a mustache of stiff black bristles. But still the eyelid hadn't closed. Worse yet, it had popped open wider, giving her a RuPaul meets Captain Jack Sparrow look. Gatlin took another deep snort of embalming fumes, closed his eyes, reached down and closed hers with the palm of his hand.

A quick shiver and he was done.

He opened his eyes.

Better... except for that mustache.

Gatlin plucked it off, resolving to stick it back later if he had the chance, and he was wondering where to store it when he heard Zaza arguing in French right outside the door. Another panic moment, he stuffed the eyelash up her nose for safekeeping and yanked the diamonds out of his pocket. He pulled up the pillow and slid them underneath it. The door opened a crack. There was shuffling, jostling, low-level stuff, but it was enough for Gatlin, and he leapt in the coffin. One of those terror-fueled spur-of-the-moment things. He slammed the lid shut. Only he didn't. He banged it on his ass. The lid wouldn't shut. This fat old cow was taking up too much room. There was a crack of light all around. They'd find him easy. The problem was the geography of it all. Gatlin's face was buried in the pillow next to hers. That meant their bellies—their zones of greatest girth—were touching. Consequently, Gatlin's butt was poking up too high. He wriggled down snakelike, Chantal's flesh wobbling under him. All it needed then was a few quick adjustments and...

The door burst open as the coffin lid clicked to. Gatlin froze in the darkness, his face wedged between her generous breasts, his belly resting on her thighs and his wanger jammed between her knees.

Please, God... don't give me a hard-on.

The voices were muffled, but Z's deep rumble was easy to recognize. Gatlin held his breath, straining his ears.

Was that *his* stomach rumbling, or...

Oh Lordy...

That had to be the weight of his chest flattening her belly and moving stuff around in there, posing the critical question: how far would that stuff move? Gatlin speculated nervously, mumbling inaudible curses at the French. *Don't they empty it out?* The creators of the bidet! You'd expect them to have all sorts of equipment for that kind of work.

The voices faded to silence and Gatlin was about to crawl out of the coffin when the voices returned. But this time, Zaza's voice wasn't among them. There were other noises too. Clunking and banging sounds. Gatlin paid them little concern. The big threat, Zaza, was gone. The Frenchies didn't bother him. If they found him, so be it. They'd squawk a bit, say *sacré bleu* a few times, and that would be it. The only problem would be the gems. If he made a grab for them, they'd think he was stealing them and get the police. So he stayed put and rested. Chantal was more than comfortable once her belly quietened down, and that mélange of expensive perfume and embalming fluid had a certain hypnotic allure. It reminded him of the Witch and her pheromones. He'd dismissed all that brain control stuff as nonsense, yet here he was sharing a coffin with another woman, and one with massive tits, but all he could think about was Felicity Drillbit. He yearned for her still, even after they'd fought and she'd shot a gun at him, he still...

When Gatlin woke up, the first thing he did was bang the back of his head on the lid of the casket. Of course, he didn't know that was what it was. In that bleary netherworld between asleep and awake, all he knew was the spongy, smelly cold beneath him and the suffocating darkness. He threw his arms aloft, banging the lid open wide and bellowing a primordial grunt. His first vivifying whiff of oxygen brought it all back in a rush.

He stumbled out of the coffin and collapsed on the floor, panting. As minutes passed, his eyes adjusted to the gloom. He wasn't in total darkness. There were slits of windows high up on the wall and a glow of ambient city lights filtered through their frosted glass. But it was precious little to see by. It was night and the world's most famous death shoppe was closed for business. He pulled a Zippo from his pocket and lit it up, then stood up, feeling a little braver with his own flame. He went to a strip of switches by the door but thought twice before turning on the lights. There had to be a guard or night watchman somewhere around. He'd be safer in the dark, waiting for daylight. It wasn't far off, and escape would be much easier when there were people around.

He went to take a peek at Chantal but backed off. He'd have to look at her sooner or later to get the diamonds out, but no way was he going to do it by the flickering light of his Zippo. The shadows created by its wandering flame were already freaking him out. He shut the lid on Chantal's coffin so he wouldn't be tempted to look. It was only then that he saw the other two coffins and remembered the sounds he'd heard after the cemetery staff had finally persuaded Zaza to leave. He checked one warily, glancing out of the corner of one eye to minimize the impact, but it was empty. So was the other one, a recyclable box, the bio model beloved by coffin flies. Gatlin went back to the first one he'd inspected. It was a cheap job compared to Chantal's, but it was wood at least and nicely lined, clearly the most comfortable of the two. But it had the disadvantage of being closest to the door. If someone burst in suddenly, he'd have no chance to do anything other than say *"Bonjour."* So he went back to the bio-box at the other end of the room. This would give him the most time to react in the event of an unexpected arrival. He was planning on avoiding that by maintaining a vigilant wakefulness. But all things considered, the bio-box was the best choice.

He clambered inside and checked his watch, squinting at its luminous dial. A couple of hours to go... just enough time to lie back and plan a successful morning based on the two essentials, picking up the diamonds and dropping off everyone's radar, especially his pursuers, a category that was ballooning by the hour. The Witch, Dimo, Zaza and now the old man too. The chances of the Ferret being the forgive-and-forget type were slim, and he, or she, or whatever... had to be itching to pay back that Liverpool kiss Gatlin had given him.

Nursing such thoughts, Gatlin dozed on and off.

And as he dozed, Miriam Blum, aka Felicity Drillbit, looked at herself in the dressing table mirror.

What a mess!

She ran her fingers through her cropped black hair, her eyes back on the dressing table top and its contents, her blond wig and her box of tricks where she stored her colored contact lenses, her nails, her... she went back to the mirror and stared into her own bland brown eyes, wondering who the real person was as her hand ghosted up to her mouth and she chewed on what was left of her real nails. For a few days, she'd better stick to this *au naturel* look. No one could possibly mistake her for that batshit-crazy bitch who'd shot up the cemetery.

But how depressing!

Not that the look was so awful, although it truly was. The hurtful part was the feeling that came with it. Absent those lustrous locks, those hypnotic eyes and threatening talons, and especially the chutzpah boots, she felt like Clark Kent coming naked out of a phone box after his alter ego had just saved the world. She had a fallback outfit for moments like this, her Red Woman look with the flaming hair and ice-blue eyes, but she didn't have the strength to carry it off. Emotionally and psychologically, she'd shot her wad on getting those diamonds, and although theoretically that still might happen, she didn't hold much stock in theory. Especially one dependent on a dumbfuck like Dimo.

She picked up her wig, noticing the gun underneath. Felicity was into guns. Miriam wasn't. She went to the wall safe and stashed it next to their money. Of course the word *their* was something of a misnomer, a placeholder for the word *her*. It was a pittance compared to the prize she'd missed out on, but at least it was enough to get her started again.

The sound of a vehicle pulling up outside had her hurrying to the window. Their hotel was in a shabby cul-de-sac with little traffic, and besides, Dimo was well overdue. She watched him hobble from the taxi to the hotel, his head bandaged and his arm in a sling. So much for the *Dimo might* theory. She packed away the wig and the other accoutrements of her alter ego and sat on the bed.

"Hi, honey," she said as he stumbled through the door, his jaw easing open in silent exclamation at the sight of her. "What happened to you?"

"What happened to me? What happened to *you*?"

"Oh, this." She shrugged at her new look. "It's a disguise. I cut off my hair and dyed it, and these brown eyes are contacts. Pretty neat... eh?"

"You look like my mother—"

"That's good—"

"After that train hit her truck."

Miriam sucked it up. No point in arguing the toss.

"So what about you? Don't tell me Gatlin did all that."

"What! Are you crazy? That wimp."

"So who?"

"Not who but what."

He seemed to get stuck at that point, his eyes wobbling around between his bandaged head and his plastered nose.

"So...?" she said.

"It was a truck."

"Wow... what are the chances of that? Just like your dear old mom. Must run in the family."

"No, she hit by train. Driving truck. Is different."

"Did you get the plate number?"

"What is this?"

"The license. The tag. Maybe we could get an insurance claim going."

He snorted. But something went wrong—his usual manly grunt transformed into a wheeze from an asthmatic pig. He grabbed his nose as blood seeped through the dressing.

"They sewing my nose... that truck drag me for ten kilometers."

"But no sight of Gatlin on the way?"

"He attack old man and take flowers. I chase. But truck problem..." He waved at his face.

"What old man? What flowers?"

He shrugged. "Old man with white flowers."

Felicity turned it around in her head a few times but couldn't make sense of it. An old man? That wasn't in the script. Still, the flowers fit. Could that crazy Brit have blundered his way to a fortune?

She stood up. "Do you want me to get you a drink?"

"I get... I get. Not beer. Need special something." He went out the door, returning ten minutes later with a bottle of... "Rakia," he said, waving the bottle with his good arm as he kicked the door closed behind him. "Bulgarian brandy. I get it from Krum." His mood seemed a lot better. Most likely, he'd already knocked one back with his hotel manager buddy. The two of them went way back in the old country, so Krum had conveniently dispensed with the usual hotel formalities, like copying guests' passports.

"Oh, honey, I can't drink that shit... it's too strong."

"I make you nice tea with little bit. We need after this day." No argument about that. "Then we sleep." He fiddled with the hot water and tea bag. "Dimo tired. No boom-boom. Sorry."

What a fucking disappointment that was. She could barely contain her joy. And so twenty minutes later, she was sipping her tea with a shot of rakia and listening to him snore at her side. That was new—the snore—evidently one of the side effects of his truck-facilitated nose job. She wondered about that. It was certainly no truck, and despite Gatlin's heroics in besting them both at the Jim Morrison tomb, she couldn't see him doing damage like that to a hulking brute like Dimo. Whatever... she was too tired to care. She slipped the phone under her pillow and turned out the light.

The Ferret had a question too...
Was a handful of painkillers enough?
It was back in its lair, staring at its mashed face in the bathroom mirror. It took a breath and held it, then set its nose with a click and a scream. Pain ricocheted around its skull, triggering horrifying images: that monster's potbelly pinning it to the floor, his face inches away, his demonic grin stretched between batwing ears.

The Ferret wanted to throw up again but tightened its throat to hold it down. It could not afford to lose the painkillers. If it could control this pain, it could think straight. Okay, so one more job, the change of plan inevitable. Rump's death was to be the final act of its distinguished career, but now another name had joined the list. That man, that creature, that satanic entity had to die. The Ferret tended its wounds and drank coffee with lots of sugar and milk. The diamonds were gone. Someone had made a big mistake. Screwing with the Ferret was a very short-term policy.

A bell sounded. Someone at the gate.

The Ferret checked the video on the intercom—a woman in jeans and a leather jacket. It was an outfit that might have been scruffy on someone else but so obviously wasn't on her. The Ferret was intrigued. What was a classy woman like that doing in this crummy neighborhood? More especially, what was she doing knocking at this door? The woman rang again, long and hard, and this time she wasn't just standing there. She had her face right up against the camera.

"I know you're in there," the woman said to the intercom. "This is Sea Urchin. I saw what happened in the cemetery. It's a mess. I sent my agent after that man. If he recovers the diamonds, I will get them to you." The woman paused. "The link between us... we can't trust it anymore. I'm taking a big chance here. I ask you to do the same. I'll pay you again if that's what it takes, but the John Thomas must die."

Sea Urchin.

That hit the Ferret like the right key in the right lock. So this was its employer. A woman. A rich woman with a grudge against the US president, and the balls to do something about it. The Ferret realized then that the diamonds were not important; the crown was a mere indulgence. Its retirement fund had long ago been overfunded.

The woman continued, a plaintive tone in her voice. "I don't expect you to come out here and chat. But I need to know. Send me a sign. I'm not going to go away until you do."

The Ferret was feeling better, relatively speaking, functional at least. The painkillers had clicked on and that was part of it. But there was something else, something personal here. The people who hired the world's greatest assassin were always ghosts. But here was a real person, an aggrieved woman. The Ferret was hardly given to self-analysis, but this was a no-brainer. This woman was the Ferret's twin, another human being fueled by hate. She wasn't an enemy. She was a kindred spirit. She wasn't a risk. She was an inspiration. The Ferret pulled out its phone, opened a deepfake voice app and selected the voice of President John Thomas Rump.

"So you want to bump me off, eh? That's very nasty. You're a nasty person. Very sad."

The Ferret watched wide-eyed. It hadn't had so much fun in... well, ever. The woman bounced back from the intercom, her face blank with shock. But she was smart, catching up in a heartbeat, a smile dawning on her face as she stepped back to the mike with a chuckle.

"That's right, you son of a bitch," she said. "I want you dead. And I've found the perfect person to make that happen."

"I'm sorry," Zaza blurted out as soon as Eve's call came through. "I failed you." He'd rehearsed his mea culpa as he waited for her, sitting at a bar, sipping a Kronenbourg. He'd laid the grief on a bit thick, but he wanted her to have no doubts about how gutted he was to announce mission failure.

"That's okay. I made contact. It's back on."

"But what about the—?"

"We'll make another payment. We set up a contact protocol. Me and him. No third parties. He insisted."

"That's crazy. You can't—"

"Not now, Zaza."

"But you can't take that risk. Going to meet an assassin with a pile of money. I can't let you. I'll—"

"Zaza..." He backed off. "You're right. We'll work something out."

"So I can deliver the new payment."

"We'll figure out something. Let's talk later. We'll leave for Normandy tomorrow. So get some rest now. I'll see you then."

The call done, he looked around the bar numbly. It was the same place where he'd been guzzling his beer only minutes before, warm colors, warm hearts and the buzz of alcohol-fueled conviviality. Now it was a bleak alien landscape, threatening and dangerous.

It's back on.

Her words echoed endlessly.

Success or failure? Would Rump die, or survive? Would the Ferret be captured, or get away? None of that mattered to him. Zaza had a crystal ball in his gut. He'd inherited it from his mother, along with his three-hundred-pound bodyweight and fists that could crush concrete. Ever since this crazy thing had started, it had been cloudy with odd flashes of the world that waited beyond the storm. One image in particular haunted him. He'd be standing all alone in a tropical hellhole, holding a can full of shit. Madame Eve would be far away. She'd get sympathy. Besides, she was French. France never extradites its citizens, and although knocking off a US president might be viewed by some as a heinous crime, most French would regard it as a proportionate riposte for those wine and cheese tariffs. Even if she was ever convicted in her home country, she'd end up in a five-star prison with her own gourmet chef and wine cellar. Poor Zaza was a Muslim with a French citizenship application still pending. And as a Turk of Kurdish ancestry caught in the willy-waving war between Rump and his Turkish counterpart, his chance of a sympathetic hearing was nil. Worse yet, they'd uncover Beverly's defection to ISIS, unless by some stroke of luck, she'd already been beheaded. God forbid she'd had a *Road to Damascus* moment at the border. What if MI6 flipped her and she said she'd been brainwashed by her Muslim husband, forced to take the veil and join the terrorists?

Zaza pulled himself back from the abyss of dark thoughts. He had to stop this. But what to do? If he bailed on Madame Eve at this late stage, it would not only cost him his job but turn him into a wimp in her eyes. Besides, it probably wouldn't protect him from prosecution in any case.

Gatlin?

Was he still hiding somewhere in that crematorium? Did he still have the diamonds? If so, he could get the diamonds as an insurance policy, or even somehow stop the assassination.

But how?

The storm cleared and a face emerged in a clear ball of glass. Zaza's last hope...

Gatlin!

SEVENTEEN

Gatlin continued to doze on and off in his bio-box coffin way through dawn, and it was during one of the "doze on" moments that a loud noise awakened him with a start, a bang so loud that he sat up with a jerk in what would have been his first successful sit-up in decades were it not for his face smacking the coffin lid after traveling a mere three inches.

Mystery.

Who closed the coffin?

He'd left it open.

Surely they'd noticed him lying in it. Did he really look so bad that some garlic-chewing cemetery geek assumed he was its rightful occupant?

Typical French.

If I'm dead… where's the bloody paperwork?

They wouldn't care. Bit of paperwork missing… they'd fudge over it. This was a corpse factory, and like any industrial plant, shit happened. They'd fiddle the books later after the one-thousand-degree oven had reduced everyone to pretty much the same thing, a bit more ashes in this one and a bit less here. Who's going to notice?

French voices. People in the room.

Some sort of dispute.

Maybe… how to do *le fudge*.

Then the sound of the lock sliding home on his coffin lid.

Gatlin remembered the latch on Chantal's coffin, a wimpy affair, even on a quality casket like hers. So he'd have no trouble bursting out of his cheapo bio-box. With that comforting thought in mind, he just listened, the incendiary implications of being locked in a coffin in a crematorium not yet graphic enough to trigger a red-zone panic. After some banging and shuffling in the room beyond, the dispute faded out into the corridor and there was silence. Gatlin seized the moment and made his move. Not a big one, it must be said—a few inches was as far as he got. He composed himself.

Don't panic.

Thank God he'd picked a bio-box. All he had to do was... he punched the lid, but with not much room to take a swing, it didn't do much. Plus it hurt. He tried again, and an incremental tick in the panic index accompanied another failure. Too bad he didn't have his Swiss Army knife. This was exactly the sort of situation it was designed for, plus he'd finally get to use that worthless can opener that no one else on the planet had yet used. The only tool he had on him was his trusty Zippo lighter. He took it out.

Wait a minute...

This was a solution that came with serious caveats.

For example, flames burn oxygen, and he'd learned from his soiree with Chantal that coffins have a tight seal and a limited supply of O_2. He immediately dismissed this overly technical concern in favor of a far more mundane consideration. He'd be burnt to a crisp way before he'd suffocate. Setting up his own low-tech crematorium inside the more grandiose Père Lachaise affair was the real risk. But what if he was careful and used the flame dexterously to singe a panel in the lid so he could bang it out and reach the latch? He'd seen similar things in movies using a blowtorch. So there was no reason to believe it wouldn't work. He flicked the Zippo on for a second, just long enough to singe a spot down by his hips on the right. He was determined to do this scientifically, and the first step was to mark the four corners of the panel he planned to burn out. He passed the lighter across to his left hand, a bit more tricky this one as he was right-handed, and... click.

Nice one.

Aargh...

The worst thing about dropping a Zippo when locked in a coffin was that the flame continued to burn, and the second-worst thing (or the *worse* thing for those stuffy about grammar) was that cremation coffins were highly flammable. Gatlin's recognition of all of the above—to his credit—took less than a zillionth of a second, getting booted aside by another acutely relevant observation—his jacket had soaked up enough of Chantal's alcohol-based embalming fluid to fire up a furnace. The whole coffin lit up like a torch and rolled off the table with Gatlin exploding out of it as it broke up on the floor. He ripped off his blazing jacket and tossed it aside. Two men witnessing it all screamed. Then one of them doused him with a fire extinguisher while the other grabbed a fire ax and approached him menacingly, like he'd seen well enough late-night movies to know how this one had to go.

"Je ne suis pas zombie." Gatlin's schoolboy French to the rescue. *"Je suis anglais."*

They froze, clearly uncertain. English or zombie? In the home of the guillotine, did it really make that much difference?

The extinguisher man had doused the flaming casket at this point, so Gatlin was getting their full attention. *"Je suis rosbif,"* he added, using the French "roast beef" pejorative for the English and chortling to lighten the mood. That wasn't easy. Those flames had not done lasting damage, but he wasn't going to need a haircut or shave for a while. The Frenchmen didn't catch the humor, and Gatlin gave up on trying when he saw the empty table behind them...

Chantal was gone.

"La madame," he said, pointing to the empty tabletop. *"Où est Madame Chantal? Le coffin..."* And finally, giving up on his French, "Where's the fat lady?"

The two men remained dumb, one aiming the fire extinguisher and the other hefting his ax like he still might need it, *rosbif* or not. Gatlin took the hint and bolted for the door. No one pursued him, and he ran down the corridor and burst through the exit door, breathing fresh air at last. Theoretically anyway, with the night-in-the-morgue odor encasing him like an envelope, finding fresh was a struggle.

The ghost of Chantal...

He had to find her before the unthinkable happened. That was too horrible. After all he'd been through.

Think!

A rich old lady like that was sure to have a ceremony. There'd be a service, music, relatives. If he could get close... join in the congregation. He'd be her English cousin, her secret one, and his lateness and unkempt appearance were due to a traffic accident involving his vehicle and a truck carrying perfume and embalming fluid. He'd get a bit emotional, cause a scene and somehow grab the gems.

But where was she?
Music...
And to Gatlin's ears, it truly was...
Non, je ne regrette rien... the voice of Edith Piaf singing the Gallic karaoke and funeral favorite, the French equivalent to Sinatra's *My Way*.

Edit Piaf again... a magical sign, if ever there was one. The Little Sparrow was Witch's diamond grave.

Quelle ironie!

Gatlin took off at full speed and found Chantal's service in full swing, inasmuch as funerals can swing. A dozen or so people in total, a miserable turnout with a few whimpering, and no one at all bawling. Obviously not a popular girl, our Chantal, although with all that cash to divvy up, her popularity was probably at its zenith. Gatlin took all that in the instant he hit the open doorway. But that wasn't what stopped him dead. That was the coffin. It was closed. Gatlin was counting on one last hug of cousin Chantal to slip his hand under the pillow.

Now what?

The music stopped and the priest recited an incantation, waving his arms above the coffin. When he stepped back, the music started again. But no more sweet Little Sparrow stuff, this was Queen's "Another One Bites the Dust" at ear-busting volume, and just before the sound jacked up, you could hear the rumble of machinery as curtains drew back, a steel panel in the wall opened and rollers edged the coffin towards a wall of flames.

"Cousine Chantal..." Gatlin screeched and ran down the aisle. Heads spun and the priest stopped tapping his foot in tune with the beat. One look at Gatlin and he seized a cross, brandishing it in front of him, both

hands clenched. Muffled under the rock beat, Gatlin could hear a few protests. He ignored them and made it to the coffin unmolested. He unlatched it in a jiff thanks to his recent coffin-tech training.

Movement behind him... and hollering so loud he could hear it even over that thumping bass line.

He blocked it all off. All he had to do was open the...

"Ugh..." He jerked back the moment he looked inside.

Who did that to her?

Chantal had always been a rather severe-looking lady, but Gatlin had dismissed that as par for the course. She was, after all, dead with little hope of a second opinion changing that diagnosis.

But how did...?

It all came back to him in an ugly flashback—his hasty exit from the coffin. He'd leapt out, or rather, levered himself out by grabbing two handfuls of... what exactly? That debate would run in clerical circles at Père Lachaise for many months, and Gatlin preferred not to get bogged down on the detail. Needless to say, those fateful handholds had undone the good work of the mortuary makeup artists and meant that the quirky RuPaul-meets-Captain-Jack-Sparrow look he remembered so fondly had become Freddy Krueger meets Leatherface.

"*Maman*...," a tearful voice was shrieking in his ear. It was the first Gatlin noticed of the big man standing at his right shoulder.

"*Quelle horreur!*" said another big man, this one standing at his left shoulder. Uncanny, that. Two identical men with bulging shoulders, barrel chests and tree-trunk necks squeezing up against him like bookends. Gatlin looked back and forth between them.

Same everything. Same bristly black buzz-cut hair, same pancake noses and cauliflower ears. They held the coffin, sobbing in sync and shuffling along with it as it crept towards the oven door. Gatlin shuffled too, although not a lot of choice in that being as he was wedged between them. So these were Chantal's boys. What were the chances? The progeny of her big belly. Twins. Rugby players with hunks of muscle and years of experience in how to hurt people. He looked down at Chantal and up at the encroaching flames. He could feel the heat. Only seconds to go. An awkward moment to be sure, and probably not the ideal one to rifle through her coffin.

Would a farewell kiss be acceptable?

Why not? The French are a renowned kissy lot.

"Ma chérie..." He bent over, stopping with his face inches from hers. This was going to take more courage than he'd anticipated, not to mention herculean sphincter tightening. The Freddy Krueger effect. He closed his eyes, one hand surreptitiously...

"Vous!"

Now Gatlin was somewhere else. Not exactly sure how he got there. He was still between the twins, but a yard or so off the coffin. He was facing one of them and the other was behind him, holding him by the scruff of his neck.

"C'est lui," the behind-him twin bawled, his voice hitting Gatlin like a karate chop. It's him... Gatlin's schoolboy French filled in the translation box. As he went to protest, Queen's thumping beat stopped and filling the emptiness of sound was the booming voice of the other twin. Who aimed an accusing finger at Gatlin and said, *"C'est vous, la goule qui a fait ça."* Gatlin got the ghoul part loud and clear, but as he struggled

to break free of the steely fingers holding his neck, he was hoisted up and slammed down onto the rollers, the coffin now having vacated a space and almost reached its destination. The priest was still crunched in the corner, hiding behind his cross. The mourners, or *the mob* as Gatlin saw them, were on their feet, howling something that got lost in translation. Something they animated with waving fists and angry faces.

With a twin on each arm, pinning him down, he edged closer to the flames.

Meanwhile, the soundtrack rolled on, a change of mood and one of Gatlin's favorites, "You Can't Always Get What You Want." He had fond memories of the Stones classic from his youth, although clearly that was a souvenir about to be recast in a darker light.

With escape not an option, he closed his eyes and relaxed, opting for the cup-half-full approach. Weird, really, the way it all panned out. After so many twists and turns, he was finally going to end up with the diamonds, albeit in a commemorative urn. He'd never believed in ghosts, the afterlife and such, but it was impossible to discount some netherworld meddling here. Could it be that during the night he'd spent with Chantal, his face buried in her boobs and his wanger trapped anxiously between her knees, he had somehow aroused her, and that her ghost-whispering had architected this moment in order that they could spend eternity together, their ashes twined in a box? It was romantic, really—a boy-meets-girl story from *The Twilight Zone*.

Bam!

One arm was free, then *bam* again, and so was the other.

Gatlin struggled to get off the rolling track, his arms slipping from under him, when he was yanked off it and dumped on the floor. The mob was silent now, staring dumbstruck at his savior. Zaza stared back, beckoning Gatlin, who got the message and stood up shakily. The twins were lying some way off, one crunched against the wall next to the cowering priest, the other lying on his back with his mouth wide open. Z grabbed a fistful of Gatlin and walked to the door. No one stopped them, for obvious reasons. Outside, Zaza dumped him on his backside on a patch of grass as soon as they'd reached the cover of trees.

"Where are they?"

Gatlin pointed back towards the crematorium's chapel but said nothing. Zaza's face fell.

"The coffin?"

Gatlin nodded. "But I have a plan. All we have to do is find out where Chantal lived, then break in and steal the urn. Or they might even stick it in the what's it..." he waved his hand towards the columbarium. "That'd make it real easy. I'll even give you a small cut."

Zaza looked troubled, his face riddling up with it. But then it passed. His face brightened and he said, "Let's go get some breakfast."

And so they trudged off with Gatlin shrugging off the past. All of it... aches here, and pains there, that macabre overnight and the fortune won and lost. He dumped it all, his stride jaunty, walking his way through a *Casablanca* flashback... *Zaza, I think this is the beginning of a beautiful friendship*.

Finding Gatlin had been easier than expected. All Zaza had had to do was follow the noise. As for his hallucinatory *histoire* concerning the fate of the diamonds, from anyone else it would have merited a beating. But from Gatlin, it was not just plausible but undoubtedly true. This was only the second time they'd met, but their two encounters, plus Gatlin's video performances in the cemetery, had been enough to convince Zaza that Gatlin was a character to whom the word *normal*, in any context, did not apply. He was like a top-secret weapon developed in an X-Men warfare lab, a Soft Terminator. His special power? Stealth wrecking. On the surface, he was a loser, a dummy. That was the stealth part, a deflector shield protecting his core functionality.

Viral chaos.

Just pick the target and get him involved. Any which way would do. With Gatlin on board, any mission was doomed, and not just to failure but to nose-in-the-dog-doo mortification. And if ever such a skill was needed, it was now. Somehow, Zaza had to find a way to stop Madame. Much as he admired her brains, her beauty, her class... and yes, her ass, if this dumb project didn't stop, they'd both be in a penitentiary nightmare instead of a happy-ever-after Hollywood ending.

The two men settled at a window table in an almost-empty café, and Zaza ordered croissants and coffee.

"Thanks for the breakfast," Gatlin said, dunking his croissant. "But I really don't have the diamonds in case you're thinking about beating it out of me. If I did, I'd tell you. I'm a well-known coward. I even have references."

Zaza waved his hand like he was batting off a fly. It was time to move on. Those diamonds would not end up, as Gatlin had surmised, on the mantelpiece of some Parisian apartment but in the pocket of some crematorium worker. Burning bodies leaves bits of bone and prosthetic metal. All that gets sieved out, the bones crushed and mixed with the ashes and the metal recycled with funds going to "good causes." Since Moroccans were the Mexicans of France, it befell them to do all the shit work like sifting through the ashes of the dead. So the Père Lachaise cemetery would shortly be getting resignations from guys called Mohamed or Abdislam.

"There's something more valuable you're about to lose."

"There is?"

"Your freedom... maybe even your life."

"How's that?"

"When was the last time someone assassinated a US president and got away with it?"

Gatlin finished chewing his pastry and wiped his mouth on a napkin.

"Forget it. There never was any assassination. It was all fake... a setup. They wanted to trap your boss."

"They? That crazy woman?"

"The Witch..." Gatlin went on to explain how Felicity Drillbit had recruited him.

"But if it was all fake, who was that old man?"

"I thought he was just some lucky bugger who took a liking to the flowers, but he shot at me and there was something really odd."

"Like...?"

"He was a woman."

Zaza took out his phone and pulled up the video from earlier, zooming in on the old man. He showed it to Gatlin.

"Seriously?"

"It was a movie mask. I ripped it off. The Ferret is either a woman... or a very unusual man."

A woman?

Zaza batted it all around in his head—the disguise, the gun, the slick message left on the poet's grave—and waited until Gatlin had finished his breakfast before sharing his news.

"That old man-woman person was the Ferret. My boss followed them, and they agreed to kill the president of the United States. The Ferret never fails. So after the assassination, the biggest manhunt in the history of the world will take place. Manhunt, not womanhunt. It will not find the Ferret or my boss. It will find you and me. We'll get the worst of it. Even if they catch the Ferret or my boss, smart lawyers will tell them to save their own asses by turning on us. They'll say, *pin it on the Muslim Turk and that mentally deranged loser with the big ears.*"

"I'm not mentally deranged."

"You're right. But you do have a certain something, and it's definitely not something anyone else would want. Or anything a jury would accept as... but I'm getting ahead of myself. You'd never even get to court."

"Why wouldn't I?"

"Because you robbed the world's best assassin and busted them up by the sounds of it. So you're already on their hit list. Plus... remember Kennedy? Lee Harvey Oswald didn't make it to a jury and neither did the guy who shot him."

"I remember... Jack Ruby. *Bang-bang.*" Gatlin looked down into his empty coffee cup and Zaza left him to ponder his fate. "I'm too young to die," he said when he looked up, "and too old to go to jail."

Zaza nodded. So far so good. Gatlin remembered the Kennedy killing. Of course he did. Everyone alive back then remembered it. TV was the new gizmo and those video clips had gotten played over and over. This was the moment. Zaza had made his pitch, and judging by the terrified look on Gatlin's face, he was now ready to join the Zaza Hassan save-our-asses club.

"What if I told you I could stop the assassination—with your help—and make you rich at the same time, would you be interested?"

"Is that a trick question?"

"I'm going to make the second payment in Normandy right before the hit takes place. So all you have to do is rob me. Then the Ferret gets no money and there's no assassination."

"Rob you... what with? An RPG?"

"A gun."

"Don't have one."

"Your old boss does."

"We've had a falling-out."

"That gun battle in the cemetery? When you update her with her new life expectancy forecast, I'm sure she'll write it off as a misunderstanding. Plus, even three ways, it's a lot of money."

"Three ways?"

"Don't you think I deserve a cut?" Zaza was confident they'd rip him off, but for appearance's sake, he had to be a stakeholder.

"Couldn't I use a fake gun?"

Zaza shook his head. "There needs to be a bullet fired into a vehicle or something, for the sake of credibility. Besides, even though she doesn't work for the CIA, she must be in touch with someone important in the US administration. How else would she have—"

Gatlin's phone rang. He took it out and checked the caller.

"Talk of the Witch... and she will appear."

Miriam, aka Felicity Drillbit etc., was two hours into her day before a mix of courage and desperation had made her pick up the phone. Those hours started when she opened her eyes and slammed them shut again. The blinds were open, the sunlight was blinding and her head was throbbing like...

Rakia... I will never drink that shit again.

She hollered for Dimo. "Aspirin, coffee."

No reply. Out jogging or some such.

She dozed, too lazy to close the blinds and too headachy to do anything else. But then it hit her. This was it. The perfect moment. It was all a blowout. The whole thing. The best she could do was take all their money and split. Apart from his phone loaded with headbanging muzak, he never took anything on his daily run. He even left the car keys, and she'd already packed. All she had to do was grab the money and get on the road.

She pulled herself up and sat on the edge of the bed.

Shit... that rakia is insane.

She grabbed her phone from under the pillow.

Shock one: it was almost noon and...

Wait a minute.

Shock two was in rehearsals, that paralyzing moment when expectation and reality skid off in opposing directions and the mind stretches like a rubber band but still can't latch on to either. She stood up, wobbling, and was reaching out to steady herself on the wall when the rubber band snapped.

Shock two: delivery.

That fucker Mickey Finned me.

The safe was open...

Why bother to look?

Even more hurtful, the dressing table and nightstand were bare. No wigs, no lenses... no tools of her trade, all gone. And no purse either, so no money and no passport. Thank God the phone had been under her pillow.

Woozily, she fumbled around the room, staring into the black hole of the safe before noticing something. A scrap of paper, a farewell note from Dimo.

I never forget Felicity 278. Sorry but homesick. Really miss dog.

So what was left?

A phone.

She thumbed through her messages and contacts. She was desperate for a cup of coffee but couldn't even afford that.

Benny?

But how was that conversation going to go? Besides, her thoughts kept looping back to Gatlin. Had he gotten the diamonds? On the other hand, that was a conversation with a bumpy trajectory what with that misunderstanding they'd had in the cemetery.

What if I apologize?

It was a radical thought, especially for Miriam, a devotee of the being-American-means-never-having-to-say-you're-sorry school of belief. But Gatlin wasn't American. He was a Brit. Different God. *Sorry* was a way of life for the Brits. She'd validated it personally by knocking one down on a crosswalk in Florida. Getting out of the car, she'd been expecting the worst and was accordingly well armed. But stunningly, the man had apologized and walked away. She'd been so disoriented she'd forgotten to hurl abuse at him.

Within moments, she'd hit the speed dial... and amazingly, Gatlin answered.

"Don't hang up. I'm sorry I shot you. Are you okay?"

There was a long pause and she thought she'd lost him when he said, "I'm very disappointed in you, Felix."

"I'm disappointed in me too. But I'm just glad you're okay. Whatcha doing? Counting diamonds?"

"Very funny. If that's why you called, you're out of luck."

"So what, then?"

"I'm hanging out with a friend."

"You have a friend?"

"How's Dimo?"

"He ran into a truck? Who's your friend?"

"The truck."

Miriam slumped on the bed.

The Turk? What the hell was going on?

She set all her questions aside, street instincts braking the spinning wheel in her head. The Mickey Finn fog was clearing and a word was coming into focus.

Opportunity.

She couldn't see the what or the how of it. But with no money, no clothes, no passport, and no gun, this looked like the elevator to somewhere a lot better.

"I was about to grab some coffee myself."

"Then join us... we're forming a new club. We're calling it the how-not-to-get-Lee-Harvey-Oswalded society. Maybe you'd be interested in joining."

"Lee Harvey...? Oh crap, please say you're joking."

"Did I mention... *and make a pile of dough?*"

Miriam got dressed, excited, her head suddenly clear. It was the oddest thing. But losing Dimo felt like the best stroke of luck she'd ever had. One last look in the mirror and... *fuck it, guys. This is Miriam. This is all you get, and it'll have to do.*

EIGHTEEN

Gatlin felt like... if not a million dollars, at least a lot more euros than he had in his pocket.

Why?

Miriam.

The ex-Felicity Drillbit, the former Witch of Langley, his ersatz tormentress, had accepted his invitation to dinner. And although finding a restaurant posh enough to impress her and cheap enough to support his budgetary restraints was always going to be a tough search, Gatlin pressed on regardless, walking as though he knew where he was going, regaling her with anecdotes and embellishing his night at the morgue to make it a story worthy of a Hollywood producer's attention. Predictably, it was Miriam who brought it all to a stop and Gatlin to his senses.

"You know this is the third time we've walked this street, don't you?"

"No, no... they all look the same... it's the cobbles."

"Gatlin, I'm not saying that El Raghead Chophouse doesn't exist or that it's not a fine dining establishment. But smooching that dead lady has given you what the French call a *je ne sais quoi*—" Gatlin whipped up his right arm and sniffed under it. "No, it's not just that unique toasted dead people scent, it's the whole package. The heavy metal makeup—" He wiped at his face and stared at the white shoe-polish gunk on his hand. "And the singed clothes and hair. So I was thinking... why don't we buy a bunch of hot dogs at that stand by the Metro, grab a bottle of vino, and have a fine dining session at your hotel."

My hotel!

Ding-a-ling.

So off they went in search of *les hot-dogs*, with Gatlin humming a Beatles tune.

It had to happen sooner or later, Miriam thought. She'd explained her dramatic change in appearance as a mere tactical adjustment and both men nodded approvingly, Gatlin even going so far as to say he preferred her new look. But sooner or later... *oh shit*... she could feel it coming. *The truth*. One of those lightning bolt moments she'd had only once or twice since she'd been a kid when the truth exploded out of her. Exploded mind, not dribbled.

"Dimo robbed me. He took everything, passport, money, my outfits... even my gun."

"The gun!" Gatlin leapt away from her and crouched down like he was about to launch an attack.

"I was planning to scam him, of course. But that's hardly the point. And the bastard was married. Can you believe that—"

"How're we going to shoot up Zaza's car?"

"Come on... we don't know how that's coming down. We won't know till we get there. Anyway, it's a bunch of bullshit. Why can't he just meet with us and divvy up the money?"

"Because it won't look real. Check the size of him. He wants a bullet hole in the car."

"We'll get a fake gun."

"That fires real bullets?"

They took a few more steps. Then Miriam said, "Are you still going to buy me dinner?"

Gatlin shrugged and trudged on. She took that as a yes and hurried to catch up.

"I can't go back to my hotel either. That asshole left the bill unpaid. He told that leery scumbag manager I'd be happy to work it off in the bedroom." Gatlin stopped and stared at her, then shook his head as if in wonder.

"Let's go get our dogs," he said, nodding towards the Metro station at the end of the block, "and forget that arsehole." Miriam hooked her arm in his and off they went to dinner.

Back at the hotel, Gatlin showered as she sipped cheap red wine. She was sitting at the dressing table mirror, appraising herself. It was the first time in her adult life she'd sat in front of that face—that hair, those lips, those eyes—and not done something to change how they looked. Not that it was such a bad face, she thought, just so ordinary. A good-looking woman. In high school a boy had called her handsome once and she'd slapped his face. But rightly or wrongly? Its big issue was noticeability and lack thereof. It had always seemed to her that the *real* Miriam, the one she felt on the inside, was so much more spectacular than the other real one, the one people saw from the outside, the one she was now looking at in the mirror. Time had made it worse, hammering the outside girl into a… she left her appraisal there. It was a miserable road to travel, that, its destination not entirely known, but somewhere scary.

Gatlin emerged from the bathroom in a clean sports shirt and jeans, his wash and brush-up done. He looked better than she'd ever seen him. Singeing his stringy locks in the crematorium had left him with clean-cut cropped look. As for his beer belly, all that racing around tombstones dodging bullets had done more than a week at a spa. He was never going to have a six-pack, but for a man his age...

He spread a towel on the floor and sat cross-legged on it. Miriam joined him, dishing up their modest fare as Gatlin topped up their paper cups with what he called their *plonk de floor*. It was hardly a gourmet event, but he made it special, noting the subtle interplay between the wine's saucy freshness and the wiener's understated al dente texture. Her take on it had been more like stale grape juice and a rubber doormat. But in the end, Gatlin's mood prevailed and she dumped her sad-sack face—that was never her—and laughed along with him.

"So," she said as they stuffed their sauce-strewn wrappers in the bin along with the empty bottle. "Big day tomorrow."

Gatlin nodded, subdued now, her boisterous dinner companion suddenly lost for words. He looked around the room, slid open a closet door, took a comforter and a pillow from the top shelf, arranged them on the carpet and lay down on the makeshift bed.

Miriam was standing in the bathroom doorway watching him. She'd been wondering about that. She'd run out of options. So this was it. Gatlin and his poky hotel room, or the street.

"A gentleman... after all," she said. It was supposed to be a compliment, but that wasn't how it landed.

"What?" Gatlin was wriggling himself comfortable on the floor.

"Not taking advantage of a damsel in distress."

He lay on his back and tucked his hands behind his head on the pillow and stared at the ceiling.

"I may be many things... but I'm not an arsehole."

Felicity left it there, disappearing into the bathroom and closing the door.

Gatlin closed his eyes and rested awhile. Then he rolled on his right side and, opening his eyes, he studied the fluff under the bed and what looked like a broken brush handle. He closed his eyes and listened to the goings-on in the bathroom—peeing, washing, cleaning her teeth. Then he heard her exit, the click of a light switch, creaking bedsprings and another click, followed by darkness.

He wondered about what she'd said. *Gentleman.* Was that a code word for loser? The winner got the girl. Everyone knew. He'd drooled over her when she'd been Felicity Drillbit, the evil witch. Now she was plain old Miriam and he wasn't drooling anymore. Now she wasn't a fantasy, an adults-only comic book. Now she was real, and boy, did he want her. He could have given her an ultimatum. It's the bed or the street. Would that have made him a winner? He didn't know. It would have made him feel like shit. That he did know. He rolled over, and as he did so...

"Hey, Wingnut..." Miriam's hand grabbed him by the ear, her stubby, nail-bitten fingers digging in deep. Gatlin froze, stiff as a plank. "Get your ass up here into this bed right now."

By the time Gatlin and Miriam awoke to their new world, the Ferret was already in Normandy, a few kilometers outside the village of Fesses-sur-Mer, and it being the fourth of the month, she was pedaling her bicycle along a narrow road, trimmed by verges of manicured grass backed by trees and hedges. She turned into a dirt track between trees and pulled up at a cottage so cute it wouldn't have been out of place on a chocolate box. The woods were tranquil, the birds in full song. It seemed so awful, what she was about to do, and that puzzled her. Killing had never troubled her before. Men were bugs. That hadn't changed. So why now? Surely she wasn't developing a conscience.

She put on her game face and knocked. She was a freelance reporter whose grandfather had died on the beaches of Normandy, and she had come all the way from Iowa to meet with the few surviving veterans who had living memories of that day. Notepad at the ready, she waited. Her nose? There had to be an explanation for that, and sure enough she had one, ready to be reeled off in her best American accent.

But where was Chuck to hear it?

She peered through a window into a living room with an ugly pink sofa, a coffee table made out of a kettle drum, a wood-burner and a small TV. *Modest, our Chuck*, she thought, moving on to the kitchen, where she found him, lying on the floor with two broken eggs.

She slipped on her gloves and took a tool from her bag to pick the lock but then tried the handle, and sure enough, it opened. Of course, no locks needed here. As an adopted son of Normandy, their local hero, Chuck Jones would have nothing to fear from his neighbors, and now he had nothing to fear from the Ferret either. She stood over the body, not just relieved but delighted. She'd been excused from the unsavory task of killing him, and that was clearly an omen, auguring success. The man who'd dodged a storm of lead on Omaha Beach had been felled by an omelet. The broken bowl was on the floor next to the eggs, his wheelchair nearby. She sidestepped the mess and checked the wheelchair. Yes, she'd gotten it right—the brand, the model. She had the exact same chair stashed in her truck, her ice dart air gun secreted in the left armrest. She dragged Chuck out straight and used calipers to verify his measurements... nose, chin, brow. She'd already analyzed them with facial recognition software and constructed the mask accordingly, making last-minute adjustments for her reconfigured nose. All her calculations had been spot-on, as usual. She then searched the house, finding his medals and decorations in a nightstand next to a wooden bedstead. She checked his clothes and picked a suitable wardrobe for the big day. They were of similar size, but even so, a few tucks and nips would be necessary. Finally, she checked the utility room off the tiny kitchen—a washing machine, a fridge, and a freezer. She dragged him down the bumpy half-step onto its stone floor, hoisted him up and dropped him onto a bed of frozen peas. All she had to do now was fetch her tricked wheelchair and prosthetic tools.

PART 3

A President, a Killer, a Hero and a Hard-On

"Okay, in the future, I get to rent the cars. That's all I'm saying." Miriam crossed her arms and stared out at the autoroute as it crawled under the sloping hood of their Citroen 2CV.

"This is an ironic vehicle. You want to know how many movies it's been in?"

"No. And the word is iconic. Only it's not. The word is crock. They don't call it the Tin Snail for nothing. We'll never get to Normandy in time."

"Sure we will."

"But we're staging a robbery—"

"A fake one."

"And is this your idea of a getaway car? What if there's a cop around on a bicycle? He'll run us down in seconds."

"There won't be anyone there. Just Zaza."

"In a Mercedes V-8. What are we going to do? Run him off the road?"

"Okay, so it was cheap. If you remember correctly, you modified my working capital."

"Stop complaining. You got me into bed instead. You made out like a bandit."

"Oh, lucky man..." He went to give her thigh a supportive squeeze but jerked his hand back on the wheel when the steering column started to shake.

"You bastard...," she said.

Gatlin smiled, stuck his arm out the window and tapped the canvas roof. "What about opening the sunroof? That'll make it real romantic."

Miriam chuckled despite her best efforts not to. "And stop making me laugh."

Meanwhile, a hundred miles to the east, Zaza pulled into the walled yard of Eve's villa and she appeared in the doorway. He cut the engine, stepped out and stood by the car, all very correct, his face stiff and formal. He wanted her to know the night before wasn't over. They'd had a row, and she'd refused to yield, insisting that she had to deliver the payment to the Ferret alone. So he'd lost the battle, but the war was ongoing, and he had to win. He had to sabotage this mission both to protect her and save both their asses.

As she approached, he held out the keys.

"Your car," he said. "I'm resigning. You'll need a new minder."

"Zaza, please..."

"I can't let you take that risk. If you don't—"

"Enough!" She held up her hand. "I refuse your resignation. I won't let you go. Besides, I contacted the Ferret last night and after some difficulty—"

"I get to do it?"

"I've made up the package for you already. Let's grab a quick coffee before we go"—she turned to head for the house—"and I'll take you through it. You can drop me in Fesses by that old church there."

"Not planning on a confession, I hope." Zaza's little joke was an excuse for his beaming grin. That had gone so much better than he'd hoped. His bluff had worked. She'd seen his resignation coming and headed it off. Now if only Gatlin & Company could rob a willing victim, there'd be no payoff, no dead president and no Guantanamo gulag.

"It's Romanesque—the church, really old. I'll take a few photos just like a tourist."

Better and better, Zaza thought. A tourist in a church. What could be safer? Now all he had to do was get the delivery details and relay them to Gatlin. Then everything should go like clockwork. She'd be devastated by the failure of her plan. But she'd be grateful to him too. He'd been robbed at gunpoint. What if that had happened to her? She'd be out even more money, although that had never been an issue for her. He'd be safe and so would she, and no one would be hunted by the FBI. In other words, normal service would be resumed. He sat at the kitchen table and watched her as she worked the coffee machine, every movement of her body special, his mind spinning into previously unexplored territory.

"Are you sure this is the right place?" Miriam said, shifting her head from side to side to peer through the leaves. The Tin Snail was tucked between bushes off a minor road outside the village of Fesses-sur-Mer.

"He's only ten minutes late," Gatlin said. "Here... you look." He gave her the phone and she read the message.

"So have you ever bumped a car?" she said.

"I've crashed loads of cars, and that was by accident. Doing it on purpose... I'll be a natural. I'll do a bang-up job. Trust me."

"Bumped is different. No one's supposed to get hurt. And being as we're in"—she tapped the tinny dashboard with her knuckles—"and we're bumping into the apex of German engineering with every imaginable safety feature, the risk is all ours. For example, do you know where you're going to hit him?"

"Where? I'm just going to bash into him. Roar out of this bush and *smashola*." He whacked his fist into his palm. "Then we leap out with our—"

"Don't get me started on that—"

"Then what?"

"I should do the bumping."

"You!"

"I bumped a few cars in my day. Now and again. For pin money."

"Insurance scams?"

"I have a varied skill set. And I guarantee we'll have more chance of survival if I'm at the wheel."

Gatlin took a long look at her, his elbow propped on the steering wheel, his jaw set in his cupped hand.

"Okey dokey," he said, getting out of the car.

Miriam shuffled across to the driver's side, the two steel-framed seats so close it was almost a bench seat. She fastened her seat belt as Gatlin took her place in the passenger seat and shuffled around.

"Don't forget your seat belt."

He fumbled around looking for it.

"So where are you going to bump him?" he said.

"Well, there are basically two options. Either—"

"Shit..." Gatlin yanked on the seat belt a few times before opening the door and pulling it free. Then as he looked up, he stopped and said, "Time to decide. Here he comes."

Miriam saw it too, the big Merc in flashes through the foliage as it cruised slowly towards them.

"Seat belt," she snapped, starting the engine as Gatlin slammed the door. She heard some sort of click and...

"Got it."

Option one was the fender. Hit right, the car would swerve away from them, ensuring their safety, and by matching the Citroen's toughest bit, its old-world metal bumper, against the Merc's weakest, its purpose-built fragile fender designed to absorb impact and protect the occupants, she was making a smart choice.

Bang... bang.

She'd gotten it right too, the timing perfect. The Mercedes skidded onto the verge and scraped to a halt in a line of scrub.

Only what was that second bang?

That blank was filled in by Gatlin, his chin nestling on the dashboard under a smear of blood on the windshield like an exclamation mark complete with a dot. He wasn't moving, but his groaning was a comforting sign of life.

Zaza was pacing towards them already, a brown paper parcel wrapped with a string under his arm.

Miriam got out of the car and threw up her arms in a gesture of hopelessness before waving at Gatlin, his face frozen against the glass in twisted delight.

"Where's my bullet hole?" Zaza said, pointing at the car. "This is not good enough."

"It'll have to do." Miriam was miffed. She'd done a real good job on that fender, and no one had gotten injured. Except for Gatlin, of course, but for obvious reasons, he didn't count. "Big brain has a water pistol. He thought it was an air gun when he bought it. But anyway, as you see... he's busy." She pointed at the parcel. "Is that the money?" He nodded and held it up for her to take. "It looks kind of small. What notes is it in?"

"I don't know. She packed it for me. Five-hundreds, I suppose."

"Even so..." She took the packet and ripped a strip of paper off with her teeth. "Oh... oh."

Zaza grabbed it and tore it apart, blank sheets of A4 paper tumbling from his frantic fingers. Then he stopped and glared at Miriam.

"She tricked me. She's at that church in Fesses... she..." He looked back the way he'd come towards the village.

"She's paying the Ferret?"

He nodded once, twice... with all the solemnity of the Guantanamo-bound.

Splat!

"Hand it over," Gatlin screeched from behind the open car door.

Zaza wiped the water off his face and stared at his hands. Miriam was wondering about that water too. It was pink. Gatlin was still taking cover behind the car door, his pistol aimed through its crack. His head was weaving back and forth and his eyes looked even more vacant than usual.

"Unless I can stop her!" Zaza said, ignoring Gatlin's intervention and running back to the Mercedes.

Zaza made a three-point turn and disappeared back the way he'd come in a screech of tires. Miriam checked the Citroen. It had stood up well. Great bump. But where was Gatlin?

He was lying on his back, spread-eagled like he'd been shot by a heavy-gauge water pistol. Miriam dragged him to the car, sat him up with his back against a wheel and slapped his face a few times.

"Hey...," he bawled, his eyes wobbling. She stopped whacking him and stood up, giving him a few minutes to catch up. "Howd'it go?" he said finally.

"Do we have a plan B?"

"Oh... shit."

Sea Urchin was waiting.

No surprise, that. Coming alone was a huge risk for her, but the Ferret had seen the fire in the woman's eyes. She'd pay any price, take any risk. Such was her hatred for this man. The Ferret knew that burn. The woman was standing by the grave of Claude Modin, an impressionist painter whose depictions of death were ridiculed in his day and who had died a pauper to be buried in the scruffy churchyard of this run-down chapel.

Later that day, the president would sweep into the village square on the other side of the church, where assorted toadies, selected media, and bored villagers were already assembling to witness his death. According to the schedule, released at the last minute for security reasons, the president would make a short speech to thank the mayor of Fesses, then "inspect the troops," talking to US veterans, some of them in wheelchairs, but most seated prominently in the front row of the crowd. There would be hugs and smooches and plenty of photo ops. Following that, the Secret Service would clear the square (tear gas was available), so the president could make videobites for Fox News, clutching a Bible in front of the church.

All of that was only hours away. So the Ferret had on its game face. Or rather Chuck's. And not only his face, but his hands and neck too, gnarly stuff, all veined to an exact match. He wheeled his chair up next to the woman and handed her a bunch of white lilies. The woman inspected them before propping them against the crumbling tombstone.

A bystander might have thought that she was merely assisting the old veteran who couldn't reach the tomb from his wheelchair. After that, they both stood, heads bowed, for a moment of silence. Then the woman said, "I found something special for you." She turned towards the old man and shook his hand briefly before their eyes went back to the grave. At least, that was how it looked. But the Ferret's eyes were on the item she'd passed him and that was now in his gnarly hand, an object whose beauty exceeded anything he'd ever seen.

"Not a ruby. A fancy red diamond from the Argyle mine in Australia. One point two carats." It was set in a ring, its red stone cut in a squarish radiant shape and trimmed with white diamonds. "It cost me four point two American."

The Ferret nodded hurriedly—thank God he didn't have to speak, he'd be too breathless. He pulled up his left sleeve and slipped it under the silicon of his tight gauntlet so he could feel it bite into his wrist.

The woman offered her hand a second time. "Good luck."

They shook and the woman spun in a waft of fragrance and threaded her way through derelict tombs and out of the churchyard.

The Ferret turned back towards the grave. He had time, a moment to compose himself. He ran through the kill, visualizing each step like a kicker lining up a ball with goalposts.

Three options.

His best shot. The president stops and speaks to the aging veteran. He'd be standing right in front of the wheelchair, an easy shot. One flick of his wrist and the ice pellet would be in the president's blood, melting instantly, a megadose of XRAT speeding towards his brain. Rump would take a few more steps and suffer a massive stroke, toppling onto the cobblestones like a giant timber. That last part—the walking away a few steps—was important. But since it was out of his control, he set it aside. The nightmare fate of getting crushed to death by Rump if he fell on him was a hazard he'd have to live with. Apart from that, the only risk was partial success, and that'd be the same as failure. For example, if the stroke only destroyed forty percent of his brain, he might not notice, and the public certainly wouldn't. Worse yet, with an electorate already enamored by his *shockpolitik* and anagrammatic tweets, blubbering unintelligibly could send his ratings stratospheric.

Option two was trickier, the brief shake. A momentary pause, then he'd be gone. This was why the Ferret had built the air gun into the left arm of the chair. He'd trigger it as Rump was standing there and he was shaking with his right.

Option three was the trickiest. What if he walked on by? The chances of nailing a moving target with an ice dart would be microscopic. The Ferret simply couldn't let it happen. He'd have to stop him.

But how?

He gasped, a flash of inspiration leaving him breathless. He slipped his hand under his scarf and touched the electrolarynx affixed to his throat. Yes, he'd thought of that. Realizing that a youngish voice was never going to pass for a veteran's croak, he'd practiced with this computerized voice box to be ready for option one, the conversation. But he could use it for option three too. He could start the conversation and stop the president from walking by. All he had to do was utter a few magic words, a mantra to bring the president skidding to a halt. He rehearsed the line, using muscles in his tongue and throat to generate the synthetic speech...

MAKE AMERICA GREAT AGAIN

Nice... and the subtext would give Rump a hard-on. *Even the droids are voting for me.*

The motorcade swept into the square and stopped, and Horndog exited Wheels One as Secret Service men hustled all around him and gendarmes lounged on the periphery, puffing away at Gauloises. The president surveyed the crowd, wafted his hand royally and was escorted to a podium.

What a fine fellow of a man, Gatlin thought. He was standing at the end of the bleachers next to Miriam, having passed through the security perimeter without incident, other than the confiscation of his water pistol. Rump seemed bigger in real life than on the screen and he was immaculately turned out in a generously cut blue suit with a red tie.

Gatlin made mental notes for his tailor—when he got one—noting the slimming effect of the president's loose-cut clothes. Rump was an old boy like him, but he looked so much better. The secret was in that orange glow and—Rump smiled—his American teeth, snow-white and glinting in the sun. Gatlin's were more like snow that someone had pissed on, and then taken a dump as an afterthought.

"You think it'll happen here?" Miriam said.

It was a good question and begged a second, even more pertinent one. Why were they even there? They had no plan, and they were flat broke. Gatlin's choice was the high road, beating a hasty retreat in an effort to vacate the blast zone. But Miriam was at the wheel. So she'd made the call.

"There he is—Zaza. Over there. Sitting with his Madame." Gatlin jerked his head towards the bleachers.

Miriam stared at the couple as the president droned on. "We could blackmail them."

"Who?"

"Coronata and her bulldog. She's loaded."

"But if we shopped them, we'd get arrested too."

"Ratted them out, you mean? We'll turn state's evidence. We'll get immunity."

Gatlin was familiar with the concept, called Queen's evidence in the UK, or more commonly supergrass. "Zaza saved my life. Those rugby twins were stuffing me in an oven."

"Nothing's going to happen to him or her. They'll pay us a little money. That's all. She's got plenty. CringR's a mint."

That made sense, but it didn't sit well with Gatlin. He wasn't happy about being a loser, but he was comfortable with it. Even thinking about being a rich rat made his skin itch. Then there was the second point, the pronoun thing. That *we'll* as in "we'll get immunity" could so easily change to an *I'll*.

"Think about it, anyway. And in the meantime—"

"But what about *us*? Our future?"

She looked at him, her face blank.

"We'll always have Paris," she said reassuringly. "Now as I was saying... we can bail ourselves out by making some quick cash on YouTube." She whipped out her phone. "We've got a front-row seat for the assassination of the century. We'll be rich. We can escape... go anywhere."

There it was again. That pronoun thing was starting to bug him. Gatlin was smitten by Miriam, and not so dumb that he didn't know it. He'd follow her off a cliff and then climb back up to do it again. And he admired her quick thinking and resourcefulness, it was just that—he struggled to catch the elusive thought—he'd never met a woman so treacherous that she made him feel... the word he was after was *honest*, but it had always been an elusive concept and he couldn't bring it to mind. So he set it aside. This was no time for philosophy in any case. Today's agenda was action. The president was winding up his speech, much to the pleasure of the uncomprehending locals who'd been press-ganged into the event and were no doubt missing a long boozy lunch.

This wonderful, magnificent mayor of yours—great guy by the way, the best—said to me, Mr. President, sir, the citizens of Fesses are thrilled that you're blessing our insignificant village with your presence, but they ask me why? The president paused for enthusiastic applause from the Fox News people and a disinterested ripple from the locals obeying the *applaudir maintenant* signs held up by Rump's minions. *When I heard there were some US veterans in the area who couldn't make it to the big event at the cemetery, I insisted on meeting them here, where I too have memories... different kind of famous beach, though.* He chuckled. *Hey, you...* He pointed at one of the veterans. *I saw that smile. You know what I'm talking about, eh?* He winked. *You old rascal.*

A woman suddenly appeared at the president's side, an older woman now, but no doubt a traffic stopper in her day. She leaned in close to the president's ear and hissed a message through gritted teeth. The president's face clouded with gravity and his eyes glazed. She grasped his elbow with both hands and led him off the podium, handing him off to a male flunky, who guided him towards the veterans. Gatlin surveyed the old men admiringly. Real heroes. What must that be like? Having the balls to run into a hail of bullets while your buddies were getting sliced down all around you. He envied them despite their decrepitude, the bitter fruit of survival—old age and infirmity. Some of them even looked...

Wait a minute...

The Ferret was studying the president.

Option one, two or three?

It was soon clear that the president was not making a fly-by visit. He was dawdling. Let the world leaders wait. Here was a photo op worth milking and every veteran was getting a handshake and a pat on the shoulder as a minimum. The Ferret shifted his left hand and released the safety on the air gun. Now all he had to do was touch his thumb to the reader inside the armrest and it would fire. He'd do it after the handshake as the president was reaching for that condescending...

Oh no... it can't be...

The Ferret's encroaching victim was forgotten. Standing at the end of the bleachers and edging closer was his attacker from the cemetery—there was no mistaking those batwing ears—and the man was staring right at him.

Oh my God, I...

"And this, sir, is Chuck Jones, a hero of Omaha Beach."

The bat-winged Satan disappeared, blocked out, like the sun, by the presidential bulk in front of him. Rump mumbled something. Or maybe it wasn't a mumble. Maybe that was the Ferret's scrambled brain unable to process the sounds. He stuck out his right hand and the president shook it. From here on it was all down to muscle memory. The Ferret slid his thumb towards the trigger as the president went for his pat. But at the last moment, he turned away. And so did everyone else, their attentions grabbed by a deafening screech.

Get the Ferret before it gets Rump.

The Ferret jerked his head to see past Rump, fumbling as he hit the trigger, his hand slipping off the armrest and into the line of fire.

Just a prick. Like a wasp sting.

That prosthetic skin was silicon, not Kevlar.

Was it enough to...

TWENTY

Gatlin took umbrage.

That was what started it.

Why is that old boy eyeballing me? So what if I've got big ears?

The other veterans were waiting patiently for the president to bestow his shake and anoint them with his pat. Some even got a bit of chat. Especially the leery one who shared the president's interest in Normandy's beaches *au naturel*. Rump even took a few notes while chatting with that guy. All the rest were waiting their turn, their eyes on the big man, all except the dinky vet at the far end who only had eyes for Gatlin.

"Oi... mate... whatcha lookin at?" Gatlin barked it out, summoning his best Brit loutspeak.

Miriam jerked his arm. "Shh."

He'd woken up a bunch of local dignitaries snoozing on the nearby bleachers and they were rebuking him with snotty looks, chins tilted, eyes aimed down aquiline noses. Gatlin ignored them and went back to the old vet whose obsession with him continued, worsened even, with his head sticking out on his rubbery neck, completely ignoring the president who was about to...

Rubbery neck!

Gatlin shook off Miriam's restraining arm and charged screeching. Bodies swirled and twisted, and some of them ran too. The Secret Service were all over the president, and he hit the ground with a thud, bodies piling on top of him. Other agents were rushing in from the sidelines, some with guns drawn, others their karate-chop hands at the ready. Gatlin screeched again, raising his hands to show he was unarmed before diving into a tackle. The last thing he saw before launching himself was the Ferret ripping at the rubber skin of his bloodied hand, and a gold ring with a red stone falling from it into his lap. His shoulder crashed into the old veteran's medals and the wheelchair flipped backwards. In seconds, strong arms had yanked him off and dragged him back. Others tended to the Ferret. It wouldn't take them long to discover that...

Bingo.

There it was, one excited agent calling a bunch of them into a huddle over the upturned wheelchair.

"Get the fuck off me!" the president said, addressing the mattress of bodies on top of him. Two agents helped him to his feet and he brushed his suit vigorously, but when they tried to assist he pushed them aside and, pointing his finger accusingly, he said, "Which one of you bastards grabbed my balls?" An agent whispered in his ear, not a confession evidently, but breaking news that stopped his fussing in its tracks. In fact, he stopped everything, even blinking his eyes. "He's a what? She's a what? Is it...?" He slid his hand under his throat and the agent nodded in reply. The president's face lit up, not suddenly, but gradually like a splendid dawn. Then he seemed to notice Gatlin being dragged off with much protest. He pointed at him and said, "Who's that? Bring him here." His Secret Service escort dragged Gatlin in front of the president and one of them went to speak but the president quieted him. "What's your name? Let him go." The agents did as they were told but stood so close to Gatlin he could barely breathe.

"Gatlin Fry, sir. MI6, retired. Now working as a private security operative."

"So who hired you?"

"No one, sir, I'm a"—the word was somewhere in Gatlin's maze of a brain—"a Rumperholic, sir. UK branch. I've been on the track of this monster for some time and when I heard that you were a possible target, I came here to protect you... to give my life if necessary." That last part was laying it on a bit thick, but from what Gatlin had heard, Rump liked his bullshit served solid.

"Come here, boy." Rump shooed away the protesting Secret Service agents and, putting his arm around Gatlin's shoulders, he led him up to the podium, where Gatlin saw Zaza hustling his boss away from the commotion.

Zaza bundled Eve into the back of the Merc. She was sobbing. A difficult moment. He wanted to scream with joy. The day of reckoning had come and gone, the bullets well dodged. No assassination and one dead assassin meant no investigation. Or very little. Given this president's popularity with the FBI, this failed effort was more likely to provoke groans of disappointment.

Eve cried in Zaza's arms, her face hidden in his chest.

Would she read the writing on the wall and move on? Or hatch another crazy plan? For sure he'd have to bail out then. He could never—

She pushed herself off him roughly. Her tears stopped and her eyes flared with anger.

"I hate myself," she said. Zaza frowned but said nothing. He couldn't figure this one out. She was angry alright, but at what? "How could I do this to you? I'm a bitch. You tried to stop me, you blessed angel, to save me from madness." Zaza mumbled platitudes, telling her not to beat herself up. "A monster, that's what he made me, all these years consumed with hate."

So that was it. A bit overdue, but she was coming to her senses.

"What did he do to make you so mad?" This was the other half of the conversation they'd started in the jet to Alicante and never finished.

She composed herself, taking deep breaths while Zaza poured her a brandy from the minibar. She sipped it and it seemed to calm her. He hoped it would give her the nerve she needed to finally tell him the truth about what had happened between them.

"We were an item, the president and I—at least that's the way it was going."

"You dated?"

"We had dinner and then went back to his hotel room."

"In Moscow?"

"At the pageant, yes..." Zaza's jaw was dropping at a rate of one millimeter per second with his head edging towards her at approximately the same rate. "I'd hacked the pageant computers way before the contest and *edited* certain documents relating to... a personal matter."

"Like?"

"Oh dear... I'm running out of euphemisms and trying to stay ladylike."

"I'll be a gentleman... promise."

"Gentleman." Her eyes flashed under dark lids. "It's odd you should put it like that."

"What happened back in his room? Did you make out?"

"We were getting there."

"Groping?"

"*Grabbing* is his preferred term."

"And then?"

She slugged down the rest of her brandy in a gulp that left her gasping.

"Oh hell," she said, when her chest stopped heaving. "When I hacked those application papers, I changed my birth name—"

"Whatever for? What was it anyway?"

Her eyes met his, coming up slowly, a sudden calm tinting them with sadness.

"Eric." Her voice had a flatness that Zaza didn't pick up on at first.

"That's a strange name for a..." And when he finally caught up, his face pulsed red. "You mean, you were a—"

"I edited that part too."

"And so when he..." Zaza reached his meaty paw towards her crotch but pulled up short.

"He got hell of a surprise."

"So what did he say?"

"I will never repeat that, or forget it. But his words poisoned me with hate."

"And now you're cured?"

"Hating haters is letting them win. And the worst part is how I dragged you into all this, exploiting your loyalty." Zaza snatched up the brandy bottle and upended it, his Adam's apple throbbing in and out as if counting the gulps. "I still can't figure out why you stuck by me? And now you know the truth, you must hate me." Zaza quit guzzling and nursed the bottle, shuffling his butt around like he'd just noticed how uncomfortable those darn Mercedes seats were. "I'll pay you what I promised. You'll get your dream. You can be on your way to Bodrum before sunset. You and Beverly."

"My divorce came through." He blurted it out, his voice pealing with joy. "Beverly's joined the jihad. Praise be to God. So maybe, if you think... feel that... anyway—"

"Zaza, are you okay? Your face is... and the veins in your neck are... what are you trying to tell me?"

"Meatballs, meatballs..."

Eve needed no translation. She grabbed handfuls of his shirt and ripped it open, buttons pinging wide. "Amen," she said before burying her face in the hairy mane on his chest.

Ladies and Gentlemen, the president began, *distinguished guests... and the French. They say God works in mysterious ways and we see here His blessed hand at work. This brave hero*—he patted Gatlin on the back—*risked his life to save me. An assassin lies dead*—he waved at the swarm of agents still hovering around the upturned wheelchair—*thanks to the grit of this man, a veteran who stood shoulder to shoulder with our own fearless warriors. Thanks to him, I'm alive and the... eh...*

"Ferret, sir," Gatlin said. "That's the Ferret. One dead Ferret, right there."

"Okay... but don't interrupt me when I'm in the zone in future."

"Sorry, sir."

*So where was the CIA? Those idiots. Wasting their time and your money cooking up crazy—*he stopped and stabbed each word with his finger—*there was no collusion.* Rump paused again, puffing a bit now. This CIA topic obviously pissed him off big-time, and to Gatlin that was an invitation.

"If I may, sir, my partner—my fiancée—helped me track down the Ferret. She was CIA-trained but quit due to their institutional incompetence. She's right over there." He pointed out Miriam and Rump waved her up onto the podium, and as she hurried across the cobblestones, Gatlin went for the jugular. "Sir... any chance of jobs for the boys?" Rump glanced at him and winked. "I've got something special lined up for you." After introducing Miriam as *another victim of CIA persecution and incompetence*, there was a short pause for a photo op. That started grandly with the president center stage, his arms draped around Gatlin on one side and Miriam on the other, smiling faces all around. But then it got ugly when the president wanted a *money shot* with the dead Ferret dragged up on the podium for him to pose, hunter style, with his foot on the Ferret's head. In the end, it got to shouting, and they had to send in the Rump Whisperer to get him back under control. That fractious issue resolved, he went back to the microphone.

"And now I have an important announcement. Starting as of now, Gatlin Fry, the hero of Fesses, will serve on my White House staff as an executive adviser responsible for the reorganization of the CIA and the FBI—that's basically firing people for those of you who don't know how I work—and he'll be known as the Special Intelligence VIP, or SPIV for short." There was a gasp from the audience, especially the president's team, although that was more of a scream. Stepping away from the microphone, the president called over a flunky and reeled off instructions as the man eyed Gatlin warily and confirmed each with a nod and a curt "Sir." That done, the president was whisked off and the instructed flunky approached Gatlin and Miriam.

"Sir... ma'am." He nodded to them both in turn. He was a good nodder. "My name is James and I've been assigned the post of executive personal assistant to the SPIV. It's my job to ensure that you are secure in the envelope for—"

"Envelope? Like a very big one, I hope."

"That's an expression, sir, to define the VIPs in the security bubble of the United States presidency."

Gatlin snickered and punched James on the shoulder. "I'm pulling your leg, you old wanker, British humor." Miriam laughed too. Then she slipped her arm around Gatlin's waist, secured a pinch of his love handle and twisted it hard.

"After your physical encounter here," James continued, "you may wish to recuperate and refresh. Or we can arrange for your jet to Washington immediately, so you can..."

Gatlin had heard enough. Miriam could decide all this fine print stuff. He was in the envelope. That was enough for him. The big time beckoned, and as he watched the Secret Service men stuff the Ferret into a body bag, he dreamed...

Washington... the White House.

The US president owed him his life. From zero to hero, he'd made it. From here on out, he was untouchable. He could afford to dream big. Forget that paltry Winnebago. Now he could get a Hollywood RV like Tom Cruise, the biggest they make. And he could put it wherever he wanted... he could... wait... even put it on the White House lawn.

Oh yes... it was time to dream big.

Epilogue

Where were you when it *didn't* happen?

Like the Kennedy assassination of yore, no one would ever forget where they were when an unknown hero saved President J.T. Rump from the ignominious fate of a jumbo-sized Chinese rat. Benny Capone witnessed it from his Manhattan apartment, staring at the TV, naked save for a lavender silk robe and black wool socks.

The place was a mess, half-empty boxes—tiny ones—of Italian food littered the floor. He hadn't been out for days, not since... well, you know, that misunderstanding he'd had with the president. And so he watched as the coverage rolled on.

Rump was everywhere... sneering at the groveling Macron, preening with the fawning May, and snarling at the giggling Merkel when her congratulatory slap on the back dislodged his quiff, giving him a cute Old English sheepdog look that went viral.

Benny wiped at his tears. It couldn't have gone worse.

His phone rang.

His wife.

Yes, it could.

She'd passed details of his Cayman Islands retirement fund to the IRS. Another day, he might have lost it, but not today. He grunted and tossed the phone into a box on the floor, and as it splashed in the remains of yesterday's tortellini in brodo, he got an idea.

Phone...

The First Lady might still have that burner phone he'd given her. These TV images were live, so she wasn't actually with the president at the moment. According to the schedule, they'd meet up later at the Veteran's Cemetery for the walkabout. Right now, she'd be working through her endless toilette, and as an ex-model, she did most of that herself, only calling in her makeup crew for last minute touch-ups. She'd be alone. What would she be thinking? The assassination had failed, but my hero Benny had come through for me. Benny leapt up and ran out of the living room. He grabbed his burner phone from the office and put the call through.

Voicemail.

Humpty-Dumpty sat on a wall...

He listened, his heart soaring as it all came back... that bathroom, her laughter. And she'd left him this special message, cooing it as if to a child. That had to mean...

Humpty Dumpty had a great fall
All the President's horses and all of his men
Couldn't put Humpty together again

Her voice switched gear into icy Slavic bitch mode. "So they buried him in a trash bin, and nobody ever saw him, or heard from him, or thought of him ever again." She sighed, long and theatrical. "And that was the end of Humpty."

He listened to the dial tone waiting for more, but none came. He flung the phone at the wall and grunted with satisfaction when it exploded, batteries tumbling aside and glass cracking. He marched back to the living room, kicking at boxes in a macho burst of aggression. He slumped in his TV chair, grinding his teeth, anger swirling, until an image stopped him dead.

Wingnut.

He'd seen the president's speech earlier, that idiot Fry getting a plum job in the White House, but still reeling from the failed assassination attempt, he'd failed to consider the consequences. Now here was a clip to slam home the reality of that hallucinatory moment. Wingnut was on his way to Washington. He was standing at the top of boarding stairs, waving like the resident himself, and next to him, her hand sporting a red rock ring and wafting it to-and-fro like your-royal-highness, was...

Benny dribbled, his lips trembling.

Wingnut and the Witch... in the White House. Hell's dream team. His madness and her meanness. What were the implications?

Benny went back to his office, sat at his desk and dialed out on the landline. He knew a guy—he always did—a travel agent for people interested in faraway places and keen to get there in a hurry.

He went through the usual salutations, then said, "So I've got this client... actually he's more of a friend of a friend. And he's got a few issues and he'd like to emigrate to— ... Yes, I'm sure Australia is a great place, and thanks for the suggestion. But he was thinking more along the lines of North Korea. Somewhere SEAL Team Six would have a hard time getting into— ... Timeframe? ... How about..." he checked his watch, "Twenty minutes."